con...ted.

The laughter that ripped from his throat felt surprisingly great. He'd had nothing to laugh about for far longer than he cared to remember. Several heads turned to watch him but he didn't care. He was more intrigued by the blush that spread over Raven's face.

He leaned in close. 'Do you think the angels are about to strike me down? Will you save me if they do?' he asked, *sotto voce*.

'No, Rafael. I think, based on your debauched past and irreverent present, all the saints will agree by now that you're beyond redemption. No one can save you.'

Despite his bitter self-condemnation moments ago, hearing the words repeated so starkly caused Rafael's chest to tighten. Because, knowingly or unknowingly, she'd struck a very large, very raw nerve.

'Then tell me, Raven, if I'm beyond redemption, what the hell are you doing here?'

Maya Blake fell in love with the world of the alpha male and the strong, aspirational heroine when she borrowed her sister's Mills & Boon® at age thirteen. Shortly thereafter the dream to plot a happy ending for her own characters was born. Writing for Harlequin Mills & Boon is a dream come true. Maya lives in South East England with her husband and two kids. Reading is an absolute passion, but when she isn't lost in a book she likes to swim, cycle, travel and Tweet!

You can get in touch with her
via e-mail, at mayablake@ymail.com,
or on Twitter: www.twitter.com/mayablake

Recent titles by the same author:

MARRIAGE MADE OF SECRETS
THE SINFUL ART OF REVENGE
THE PRICE OF SUCCESS

Did you know these are also available as eBooks?
Visit www.millsandboon.co.uk

HIS ULTIMATE PRIZE

BY
MAYA BLAKE

MILLS & BOON

First published in Great Britain 2013
by Mills & Boon, an imprint of Harlequin (UK) Limited,
Harlequin (UK) Limited, Eton House, 18-24 Paradise Road,
Richmond, Surrey TW9 1SR

© Maya Blake 2013

ISBN: 978 0 263 90071 2

Harlequin (UK) policy is to use papers that are natural, renewable and recyclable products and made from wood grown in sustainable forests. The logging and manufacturing process conform to the legal environmental regulations of the country of origin.

Printed and bound in Spain
by Blackprint CPI, Barcelona

HIS ULTIMATE
PRIZE

To Lucy Gilmour, for making my dream come true,
and also because I know she loves bad boys!

CHAPTER ONE

'PUT YOUR ARMS around me and hold on tight.'

The rich, deep chuckle that greeted her request sent a hot shiver down Raven Blass's spine. The same deep chuckle she continually prayed she would grow immune to. So far, her prayers had gone stubbornly unanswered.

'Trust me, *bonita*, I don't need guidance on how to hold a woman in my arms. I give instructions; I don't take them.' Rafael de Cervantes's drawled response was accompanied by a lazy drift of his finger down her bare arm and a latent heat in ice-blue eyes that constantly unnerved her with their sharp, unwavering focus.

With gritted teeth, she forced herself not to react to his touch. It was a test, another in a long line of tests he'd tried to unsettle her with in the five weeks since he'd finally called her and offered her this job.

Maintaining a neutral expression, she stood her ground. 'Well, you can do what I say, or you can stay in the car and miss your nephew's christening altogether. After agreeing to be his godfather, I'm sure you not turning up in church will go down well with your brother and Sasha.'

As she'd known it would, the mention of Sasha de Cervantes's name caused the atmosphere to shift from toying-with-danger sexual banter to watch-it iciness. Rafael's hand dropped from her arm to grip the titanium-tipped walking stick tucked between his legs, his square jaw tightening as his gaze cooled.

Deep inside, in the other place where she refused to let anyone in, something clenched hard. Ignoring it, she patted herself on the back for the hollow victory. Rafael not touching her in any way but professionally was a *good* thing.

Recite. Repeat. Recite. Repeat—

'I didn't agree…exactly.'

Her snort slipped out before she could stop it. 'Yeah, right. The likelihood of you agreeing to something you're not one hundred per cent content with is virtually nil. Unless…'

His eyes narrowed. 'Unless what?'

Unless Sasha had done the asking. 'Nothing. Shall we try again? Put your arms—'

'Unless you want me to kiss that mouth shut, I suggest you can the instructions and move closer. For a start, you're too far away for this to work. If I move the wrong way and land on top of you, I'll crush you, you being *such* a tiny thing and all.'

'I'm not *tiny*.' She moved a step closer to the open doorway of the sleek black SUV, stubbornly refusing to breathe in too much of his disconcertingly heady masculine scent. 'I'm five foot nine of solid muscle and bone and I can drop kick you in two moves. Think about that before you try anything remotely iffy on me.'

The lethal grin returned. '*Dios*, I love it when you talk dirty to me. Although my moves have never been described as *iffy* before. What does that even mean?'

'It means concentrate or this will never work.'

Rafael, damn him, gave a low laugh, unsnapped his seat belt and slid one arm around her shoulders. 'Fine. Do with me what you will, Raven. I'm putty in your hands.'

With every atom in her body she wished she could halt the stupid blush creeping up her face, but that was one reaction she'd never been able to control. In the distant past she tried every day to forget, it had been another source of callous mirth to her father and his vile friends. To one friend in particular, it had provoked an even stronger, terrifying reaction. Pushing away the unwelcome memory, she concentrated on the task at hand, *her job*.

Adjusting her position, she lowered her centre of gravity, slid an arm around Rafael's back and braced herself to hold his weight. Despite the injuries he'd sustained, he was six foot three of packed, lean muscle, his body honed to perfection from years of carefully regimented exercise. She needed every single ounce of her physiotherapist training to ensure he didn't accidentally flatten her as promised.

She felt him wince as he straightened but, when she glanced at him, his face showed no hint of the pain she knew he must feel.

The head trauma and resulting weeks-long coma he'd lain in after he'd crashed his Premier X1 racing car and ended his world championship reign eight months ago had only formed part of his injuries. He'd also sustained several pelvic fractures and a broken leg that had gone mostly untreated while he'd been unconscious, which meant his recovery had been a slow, frustrating process.

A process made worse by both his stubborn refusal to heed simple instructions and his need to test physical boundaries. Especially hers.

'Are you okay?' she asked. Because it was her job to make sure he was okay. Nothing else.

He drew himself up to his full height and tugged his bespoke hand-stitched suit into place. He slid slim fingers through longer-than-conventional hair until the sleek jet-black tresses were raked back from his high forehead. With the same insufferable indolence with which he approached everything in life, he scrutinised her face, lingered for an obscenely long moment on her mouth before stabbing her gaze with his.

'Are you asking as my physiotherapist or as the woman who continues to scorn my attentions?'

Her mouth tightened. 'As your physio, of course. I have no interest in the…in being—'

'Becoming my lover would make so many of our problems go away, Raven, don't you think? Certainly, this sexual tension you're almost choking on would be so much easier to bear if you would just let me f—'

'Are you okay *to walk*, Rafael?' she interjected forcefully, hating the way her blood heated and her heart raced at his words.

'Of course, *querida*. Thanks to your stalwart efforts this past month, I'm no longer wheelchair-bound and I have the very essence of life running through my veins. But feel free to let your fingers keep caressing my backside the way they're doing now. It's been such a long time since I felt this surge of *essence* to a particular part of my anatomy, I was beginning to fear it'd died.'

With a muted curse and even redder cheeks, she dropped her hand. The professional in her made her stay put until Rafael was fully upright and able to support himself. The female part that hated herself for this insane fever of attraction wanted to run a mile. She compromised by moving a couple of feet away, her face turned from his.

For the second time in as many minutes, his laugh mocked her. 'Spoilsport.'

She fought the need to clench her hands into agitated fists and faced him when she had herself under sufficient control. 'How long are you going to keep this up? Surely you can find something else to amuse yourself with besides this need to push my buttons?'

Just like that, his dazzling smile dropped, his eyes gleaming with a hard, cynical edge that made her shiver. 'Maybe that's what keeps me going, *guapa*. Maybe I intend to push your buttons for as long as it amuses me to do so.'

She swallowed hard and considered staring him down. But she knew how good he was at that game. Heck, Rafael was a maestro at most games. He would only welcome the challenge.

Reaching behind him to slam the car door, she started to move with him towards the entrance of the church where baby Jack's ceremony was being held. 'If you're trying to get me to resign by being intolerable, I won't,' she stated in as firm a tone as possible, hoping he'd get the hint. Aside from the need to make amends, she needed this job. Her severance package from Team Espíritu when Marco de Cervantes had sold the racing team had been more than generous, but it was fast running out in light of her mother's huge treatment bills. It would take a lot more than Rafael's sexual taunts to make her walk away.

He shrugged and fell into step beside her. 'Good. As long as you're here tormenting yourself with your guilt, I feel better.'

Acute discomfort lodged in her chest. 'I thought we weren't going to speak about that?'

'You should know by now, rules mean nothing to me. Unspoken rules mean even less. How's the guilt today, by the way?'

'Receding by the second, thanks to your insufferable tongue.'

'I must be slacking.' He took a step forward, gave a visible wince, and Raven's heart stopped, along with her feet. He raised a brow at her, the hard smile back on his face. 'Ah, there it is. Good to know I haven't lost my touch after all.'

Ice danced down her spine at his chilled tone. Before she could answer, the large bell pealed nearby. Pigeons flew out of the turrets of the tiny whitewashed church that had been on the de Cervantes's Northern Spanish estate for several hundred years.

Raven glanced around them, past the church poised at the summit of the small hill that overlooked miles of prime de Cervantes vineyards, to the graveyard beyond where Rafael's ancestors lay interred.

'Are we going to stand here all day admiring the landscape or do we actually need to go *inside* the church for this gig?' A quick glance at him showed his face studiously averted from the prominent headstones, his jaw set in steel.

She drew in a deep breath and moved towards the arched entrance to the church. 'It's not a *gig;* it's your nephew's christening. In a church. With other guests. So act accordingly.'

Another dark chuckle. 'Or what, you'll put me over your knee? Or will you just pray that I be struck down by lightning if I blaspheme?'

'I'm not rising to your baits, Rafael.' Mostly because she had an inkling of how hard this morning would be for him. According to Rafael's housekeeper, it was the first time he'd interacted with his family since his return to León from his private hospital in Barcelona. 'You can try to rile me all you want. I'm not going anywhere.'

'A martyr to the last?'

'A physiotherapist who knows how grumpy patients can be when they don't get their way.'

'What makes you think I'm not getting exactly what I want?' he rasped lazily.

'I overheard your phone call to Marco this morning… twice…to try and get out of your godfather duties. Since you're here now, I'm guessing he refused to let you?'

A tic in his jaw and a raised brow was her only answer.

'Like I said, I know a grumpy patient when I see one.' She hurried forward and opened the large heavy door.

To her relief, he didn't answer back. She hoped it was because they were within the hallowed walls of his family's chapel because she was close enough to feel his tension increase the closer they got to the altar.

De Cervantes family members and the few close friends who'd managed to gain an invitation to the christening of Sasha and Marco de Cervantes's firstborn turned to watch their slow progress up the aisle.

'Shame you're not wearing a white gown,' Rafael quipped from the side of his mouth, taking her elbow even as he smiled and winked at a well-known Spanish supermodel. But, this close, Raven could see the stress lines that faintly bracketed his mouth and the pulse throbbing at his temple. Rafael *really* did not want to be here.

'White gown?'

'Think how frenzied their imagination would be running right about now. It would almost warrant a two-page spread in *X1 Magazine*.'

'Even if I were dressed in bridal white with a crown on my

head and stars in my eyes, no one would believe you would actually go through with anything as anathema to you as a wedding, Rafael. These poor people would probably drop dead at the very thought of linking you with the word *commitment*.'

His grip tightened for a minuscule moment before that lazy smile returned. 'For once, you're right. Weddings bore me rigid and the word *marriage* should have a picture of a noose next to it in the dictionary.'

They were a few steps away from the front pew, where his brother and sister-in-law sat gazing down adoringly at their infant son. The sight of their utter devotion and contentment made her insides tighten another notch.

'I don't think that's how your brother and his wife see it.'

Rafael's jaw tightened before he shrugged. 'I'm prepared to accede that for some the Halley's Comet effect does happen. But we'll wait and see if it's a mirage or the real thing, shall we?'

Her breath caught at the wealth of cynicism in his tone. She couldn't respond because an usher was signalling the priest that it was time to start.

The ceremony was conducted in Spanish with English translations printed out on embossed gold-edged paper.

As the minutes ticked by, she noted Rafael's profile growing even tenser. Glancing down at the sheet, she realised the moment was approaching for him to take his godson for the anointing. Despite her caution to remain unmoved, her heart softened at his obvious discomfort.

'Relax. Babies are more resilient than we give them credit for. Trust me, it takes a complete idiot to drop a baby.'

She was unprepared for the icy blue eyes that sliced into her. 'Your flattery is touching but the last thing I'm thinking of is dropping my nephew.'

'You don't need to hide it, Rafael. Your tension is so thick it's suffocating.'

His eyes grew colder. 'Remember when I said weddings bore me?'

She nodded warily.

'Christenings bore me even more. Besides, I've never been good in churches. All that *piety*.' He gave a mock shudder. 'My *abuela* used to smack my hand because I could never sit still.'

'Well, I'm not your grandmother so you're spared the smacking. Besides, you're a grown man now so act like one and suck it up.'

Too late, she remembered certain words were like a naked invitation to Rafael. She was completely stunned when he didn't make the obvious remark. Or maybe it was a testament to just how deeply the whole ceremony was affecting him.

'I just want this to be over and done with so I can re-sume more interesting subjects.' Without due warning, his gaze dropped to the cleavage of her simple, sleeveless orange knee-length chiffon dress. The bold, heated caress resonated through her body, leaving a trail of fire that singed in delicate places. 'Like how delicious you look in that dress. Or how you'll look *out* of it.'

Heat suffused her face. It was no use pointing out how inappropriate this conversation was. Rafael knew very well what he was doing. And the unrepentant gleam in his eyes told her so.

'Rafa…' Marco de Cervantes's deep voice interrupted them.

Raven glanced up and her eyes collided with steel-grey ones which softened a touch when they lit on his brother.

Like most people who'd worked the X1 Premier circuit, she knew all about the de Cervantes brothers. Gorgeous be-yond words and successful in their individual rights, they'd made scores of female hearts flutter, both on and off of the racing circuit.

Marco had been the dynamic ex-racer team boss and race car designer. And Rafael, also insanely gifted behind the wheel, had at the age of twenty-eight founded and established himself as CEO of X1 Premier Management, the multi-billion euro conglomerate that nurtured, trained and looked after racing drivers. Between them they'd won more medals and championships than any other team in the history of the sport.

The last year had changed everything for them, though. Marco had sold the team and married Sasha Fleming, the racing driver who'd won him his last Constructors' Championship and stolen his heart in the process; and Rafael had spectacularly crashed his car, nearly lost his life and stalled his racing career.

The icy jet of guilt that shot through Raven every time she thought of his accident, and her part in it, threatened to overwhelm her. Her breath caught as she desperately tried to put the incident out of her head. This was neither the time nor the place.

But then, when had timing been her strong suit?

Over and over, she'd proven that when it came to being in the wrong place at the wrong time, she took first prize every single time. At sixteen, it was what had earned her the unwanted attention that had scarred what remained of her already battered childhood.

As a grown woman of twenty-three, foolishly believing she'd put the past behind her, she'd been proved brutally wrong again when she'd met Rafael de Cervantes.

Rafael's mouth very close to her ear ripped her from her painful thoughts. 'Right, I'm up, I believe. Which means, so are you.'

Her heart leapt into her throat. 'Excuse me?'

'I can barely stand up straight, *pequeña*. It's time to do your duty and *support* me just in case it all gets too much and I keel over.'

'But you're perfectly capable—'

'Rafa…' Marco's voice held a touch of impatience.

Rafael's brow cocked and he held out his arm. With no choice but to comply or risk causing a scene, Raven stood and helped him up. As before, his arm came around her in an all-encompassing hold. And again, she felt the bounds of professionalism slip as she struggled not to feel the effortless, decidedly *erotic* sensations Rafael commanded so very easily in her. Sensations she'd tried her damnedest to stem and, failing that, ignore since the first moment she'd clapped eyes on the legendary racing driver last year.

What had she said to him—*suck it up*? She took a breath and fought to take her own advice.

They made their way to the font and Raven managed to summon a smile in answer to Sasha's open and friendly one. But all through the remainder of the ceremony, Raven was drenched with the feeling that maybe, just maybe, in her haste to assuage her guilt and make amends, she'd made a mistake. Had she, by pushing Rafael to take her on as his personal physiotherapist, jumped from the frying fan into the proverbial fire?

Rafael repeated the words that bound the small person sleeping peacefully in the elegant but frilly Moses basket to him. He firmed lips that wanted to curl in self-derision.

Who was he to become *godfather* to another human being?

Everything he touched turned to dust eventually. Sooner or later he ruined everything good in his life. He'd tried to tell his brother over and over since he'd dropped the bombshell on him a month ago. Hell, as late as this morning he'd tried to get Marco to see sense and change his mind about making him godfather.

But Marco, snug in his newfound love-cocoon, had blithely ignored his request to appoint someone else his son's godfather. Apparently, reality hath no blind spots like a man in love.

Was that a saying? If not, it needed to be.

He was no one's hero. He was the last person any father should entrust with his child.

He gazed down into his nephew's sweet, innocent face. How long before Jack de Cervantes recognised him for what he was? An empty shell. A heartless bastard who'd only succeeded at two things—driving fast cars and seducing fast women.

He shifted on his feet. Pain ricocheted through his hip and pelvis. Ignoring it, he gave a mental shrug, limped forward and took the ladle the priest passed him. Scooping water out of the large bowl, he poised it over his nephew's head.

At the priest's nod, he tipped the ladle.

The scream of protest sent a tiny wave of satisfaction through him. Hopefully his innocent nephew would take a look at him and run screaming every time he saw him. Because Rafael knew that if he had anything at all to do with his brother's child, the poor boy's life too would be ruined.

As well-wishers gathered around to soothe the wailing child, he dropped the ladle back into the bowl, stepped back and forced his gaze away from his nephew's adorable curls and plump cheeks.

Beside him, he heard Raven's long indrawn breath and, grabbing the very welcome distraction, he let his gaze drift to her.

Magnet-like, her hazel eyes sought and found his. Her throat moved in a visible swallow that made his fingers itch to slide over that smooth column of flesh. Follow it down to that delectable, infinitely tempting valley between her plump breasts.

Not here, not now, he thought regrettably. What was between the two of them would not be played out here in this place where dark memories—both living and dead—lingered everywhere he looked, ready to pounce on him should he even begin to let them...

He tensed at the whirr of an electronic wheelchair, kept his gaze fixed on Raven even as his spine stiffened almost painfully. Thankfully the wheelchair stopped several feet behind him and he heard the familiar voice exchange greetings with other family members. With every pulse of icy blood through his veins, Rafael wished himself elsewhere...anywhere but here, where the thick candles and fragrant flowers above the nave reminded him of other candles and flowers placed in a shrine not very far away from where he stood—a constant reminder of what he'd done. A reminder that because of him, because of callous destruction, this was his mother's final resting place.

His beloved Mamá…

His breath caught as Sasha, his sister-in-law, came towards him, her now quietened son in her arm.

Sasha…something else he'd ruined.

Dios…

'He's got a set of lungs on him, hasn't he?' she laughed, her face radiant in the light slanting through the church windows. 'He almost raised the roof with all that wailing.'

He took in the perfect picture mother and child made and something caught in his chest. He'd denied his mother this—the chance to meet her grandchild.

'Rafael?'

He focused and summoned a half-smile. '*Sí*, my poor ear-drums are still bleeding.'

She laughed again as her eyes rolled. 'Oh, come on, my little champ's not that bad. Besides, Marco tells me he takes after you, and I don't find that hard to believe at all.' She sobered, her gaze running over him before piercing blue eyes captured his in frank, no nonsense assessment. 'So…how are you? And don't give me a glib answer.'

'Thoroughly bored of everyone asking me how I am.' He raised his walking stick and gestured to his frame. 'See for yourself, *piqueña*. My clever physiotherapist tells me I'm between phases two and three on the recovery scale. *Dios* knows what that means. All I know is that I'm still a broken, broken man.' In more ways than he cared to count.

She gently rubbed her son's back. 'You're far from broken. And we ask because we care about you.'

'*Sí*, I get that. But I prefer all this caring to be from afar. The up-close-and-personal kind gives me the…what do you English call it…the *willies*?'

Her eyes dimmed but her smile remained in place. 'Too bad. We're not going to stop because you bristle every time we come near.' Her determined gaze shifted to Raven, who was chatting to another guest. 'And I hope you're not giving her a hard time. From what I hear, she's the best physio there is.'

Despite telling himself it wasn't the time or place, he couldn't stop his gaze from tracing the perfect lines of Raven Blass's body. And it *was* a perfect body, honed by hours and hours of gruelling physical exercise. She hadn't been lying when she said she was solid muscle and bone. But Rafael knew, from being up close and personal, that there was soft femininity where there needed to be. Which, all in all, presented a more-than-pleasing package that had snagged his attention with shocking intensity the first time he'd laid eyes on her in his racing paddock almost eighteen months ago.

Of course, he'd been left in no uncertain terms that, despite all indications of a *very* mutual attraction, Raven had no intention of letting herself explore that attraction. Her reaction to it had been viscerally blunt.

She'd gone out of her way to hammer her rejection home... right at the time when he'd been in no state to be rejected...

His jaw tightened. 'How I choose to treat my physiotherapist is really none of your business, Sasha.'

A hint of sadness flitted through her eyes before she looked down at her son. 'Despite what you might think, I'm still your friend, so stop trying to push me away because, in case you need reminding, I push back.' She glanced back at him with a look of steely determination.

He sighed. 'I'd forgotten how stubborn you are.'

'It's okay. I'm happy to remind you when you need reminding. Your equally demanding godson demands your presence at the villa, so we'll see you both there in half an hour. No excuses.'

'If we must,' Rafael responded in a bored drawl.

Sasha's lips firmed. 'You must. Or I'll have to leave my guests and come and fetch you personally. And Marco wouldn't like that at all.'

'I stopped being terrified of my big brother long before I lost my baby teeth, *piqueña*.'

'Yes, but I know you wouldn't want to disappoint him. Also, don't forget about Raven.'

He glanced over his shoulder at the woman in question, who now stood with her head bent as she spoke to one of the altar boys. Her namesake hair fell forward as she nodded in response to something the boy said. From the close contact necessitated by her profession, Rafael knew exactly how silky and luxuriant her hair felt against his skin. He'd long stopped resenting the kick in his groin when he looked at her. In fact he welcomed it. He'd lost a lot after his accident, not just a percentage of his physical mobility. With each groin kick, he ferociously celebrated the return of his libido.

'What about Raven?' he asked.

'I've seen her in action during her training sessions. She's been known to reduce grown men to tears. I bet I can convince her to hog-tie you to the SUV and deliver you to the villa if you carry on being difficult.'

Rafael loosened his grip on his walking stick and gave a grim smile. '*Dios*, did someone hack into my temporary Internet files and discover I have a thing for dominatrixes? Because you two seem bent on pushing that hot, sweet button.'

Sasha's smile widened. 'I see you haven't lost your dirty sense of humour. That's something to celebrate, at least. See you at the villa.'

Without waiting for an answer, she marched off towards Marco, who was shaking hands with the priest. His brother's arm enfolded her immediately. Rafael gritted his teeth against the disconcerting pang and accompanying guilt that niggled him.

He'd robbed his family of so much…

'So, which is it to be—compliance without question or physical restraints?' Raven strolled towards him, her gaze cool and collected.

The mental picture that flashed into his mind made his

heart beat just that little bit faster. Nerves which his doctors had advised him might never heal again stirred, as they'd been stirring for several days now. The very male satisfaction the sensation brought sent a shaft of fire through his veins. 'You heard?'

'It was difficult not to. You don't revere your surroundings enough to keep your voice down when you air your... peccadilloes.'

The laughter that ripped from his throat felt surprisingly great. He'd had nothing to laugh about for far longer than he cared to remember. Several heads turned to watch him but he didn't care. He was more intrigued by the blush that spread over Raven's face. He leaned in close. 'Do you think the angels are about to strike me down? Will you save me if they do?' he asked sotto voce.

'No, Rafael. I think, based on your debauched past and irreverent present, all the saints will agree by now you're beyond redemption. No one can save you.'

Despite his bitter self-condemnation moments ago, hearing the words repeated so starkly caused Rafael's chest to tighten. All traces of mirth were stripped from his soul as he recalled similar words, uttered by the same voice, this same woman eight months ago. And then, as now, he felt the black chasm of despair yawn before him, growing ever-wider, sucking at his empty soul until only darkness remained. Because knowingly or unknowingly, she'd struck a very large, very raw nerve.

'Then tell me, Raven, if I'm beyond redemption, what the hell are you doing here?'

CHAPTER TWO

I'M NOT HERE to save you, if that's what you think.

The words hovered like heat striations in Raven's brain an hour later as she stood on the large sun-baked terrace of Marco and Sasha's home. This time the rich surroundings of the architecturally stunning Casa León failed to awe her as they usually did.

I'm not here to save you...

She snorted. What a load of bull. That was *exactly* why she'd begged Marco to let her visit Rafael in hospital once he'd woken from his coma all those months ago. It was why she'd flown to León from London five weeks ago, after months of trying to contact Rafael and being stonily ignored by him; and why she'd begged him to let her treat him when she found out what an appalling job his carers were doing—not because they were incompetent, but because Rafael didn't seem inclined in any way to want to get better, and they'd been too intimidated to go against his wishes. It was most definitely why she continued to suffer his inappropriate, irreverent taunts.

She wanted to make things right...wanted to take back every single word she'd said to him eight months ago, right before he'd climbed into the cockpit of his car and crashed it into a solid concrete wall minutes later.

Because it wasn't Rafael's fault that she hadn't been able to curb her stupid, crazy delusional feelings until it was almost too late. It wasn't his fault that, despite all signs that he was nothing but a carbon copy of her heartless playboy father, she hadn't been able to stop herself from lusting after him—

No, scratch that. Not a carbon copy. Rafael was no one's copy. He was a breed in his own right. With a smile that could slice a woman's heart wide open, make a woman swoon with bliss even as she knew her heart was being slowly crushed. He possessed more charm in his little finger than most wannabe playboys, including her father, held in their entire bodies.

But she'd seen first-hand the devastation that charm could cause. Swarthy Spanish Lothario or a middle-aged English playboy, she knew the effect would be the same.

Her mother was broken, continued to suffer because of the very lethal thrall Raven's father held over her.

And although she knew after five weeks in his company that Rafael's attitude would never manifest in sexual malice, he was in no way less dangerous to her peace of mind. Truth be told, the more she suffered his blatant sexual taunts, the more certain she was that she wanted to see beneath his outwardly glossy façade.

With every atom of her being, Raven wished she'd known this on his unfortunate race day. But, tormented by her mother's suffering, her control when it came to Rafael had slipped badly. Instead of walking away with dignified indifference, she'd lashed out. Unforgivably—

'So deep in thought. Dare I think those thoughts are about me?' Warm air from warmer lips washed over her right lobe.

'Why would you think that?' she asked, sucking in a deep, sustaining breath before she faced the man who seemed to have set up residence in her thoughts.

'Because I've studied you enough to recognise your frowns. Two lines mean you're unhappy because I'm not listening to you drone on about how many squats or abdominal crunches you expect me to perform. Three lines mean your thoughts are of a personal nature, mostly likely you're in turmoil about our last conversation before my accident.' He held out a glass of champagne, his blue eyes thankfully no longer charged with the frosty fury they'd held at the chapel. 'You're wearing a three-line frown now.'

She took the proffered drink and glanced away, unable quite to meet his gaze. 'You think I'm that easy to read?'

'The fact that you're not denying what I say tells me everything I need to know. Your guilt is eating you alive. Admit it,' he said conversationally, before taking a sip of his drink. 'And it kills you even more that I can't remember the accident itself but can remember every single word you said to me only minutes before it happened, doesn't it?'

Her insides twisted with regret. 'I…Rafael…I'm sorry…'

'As I told you in Barcelona, *I'm sorry* won't quite cut it. I need a lot more from you than mere words, *mi corazon*.'

Her heart flipped and dived into her stomach. 'And I told you, I won't debase myself like a cheap paddock bunny just to prove how sorry I am for what I said.'

'Even though you meant every single word?'

'Look, I know I shouldn't have—'

'You meant them then, and you still believe them now. So we shall continue as we are. I push, you push back; we both drown in sexual tension. We'll see who breaks first.'

Her fingers tightened around the cold glass. 'Is this all really a game to you?' The man in turmoil she'd glimpsed at the chapel seemed very distant now. But she'd seen him, knew there was something else going on beneath all the sexual gloss.

'Of course it is. How else do you expect me to pass the time?'

'Your racing career may be stalled for the moment but, for a man of your wealth and power, there are a thousand ways you can find fulfilment.'

A dull look entered his eyes but disappeared a split second later. '*Fulfilment*…how New Age. Next you'll be recommending I practise Transcendental Meditation to get in touch with my chakra.'

'Meditation isn't such a bad thing. I could teach you…'

His mocking laugh stopped her in her tracks. 'Will we braid each other's hair too? Maybe share a joint or two while we're at it?'

She tried to hide her irritation and cocked her head. 'You know something? I have no idea what all those girls see in you. You're cocky, arrogant and dismissive of things you know nothing about.'

'I don't waste my time learning things that hold no interest for me. Women hold my interest so I make it a point to study them. And I know plenty about women like you.'

She stiffened. 'What do you mean, women like me?'

'You take pleasure in hiding behind affront, you take everything so personally and pretend to get all twisted up by the slightest hint of a challenge. It's obvious you've had a… traumatic experience in the past—'

'That's like a psychic predicting someone's been hurt in the past. By virtue of sheer coincidence and indisputable reality, half of relationships end badly, so it stands to reason that most people have had *traumatic experiences*. If you're thinking of taking up clairvoyance, you'll need to do better than that.'

His bared teeth held the predatory smile of one who knew he had his prey cornered. '*Claro*, let's do it this way. I'll make a *psychic* prediction. If I'm wrong, feel free to throw that glass of vintage champagne in my face.'

'I'd never make a scene like that, especially not at your nephew's christening.'

The reminder of where they were made him stiffen slightly but it didn't stop him moving closer until his broad shoulders and streamlined body blocked out the rest of the party. Breath catching, Raven could see nothing but him, smell nothing but the heady, spicy scent that clung to his skin and seemed to weave around her every time she came within touching distance.

As if he knew his effect on her, his smile widened. 'No one will see my humiliation *if* I get it wrong.'

Afraid of what he'd uncover, she started to shake her head, but Rafael was already speaking.

'You've been hurt by a man, someone you really wanted to depend on, someone you wanted to *be there* for you.' He waited, his eyes moving to the fingers clenched around her glass. When she didn't move he leaned in closer. 'Since that relationship ended, you've decided to take the tired *all men are bastards* route. You'd like nothing more than to find yourself a nice, safe man, someone who *understands* you.' His gaze moved to her face, his incisive stare probing so deep Raven wanted to take a step back. With sheer strength of will, she stood her ground. 'You hate yourself for being attracted to me but, deep inside, you enjoy our little skirmishes because the challenge of sparring with me makes your heart beat just that little bit faster.' His gaze traced her hopefully impassive face down to her throat.

For a blind moment, Raven wished she'd worn her hair down because even she could feel the wild tattoo of her pulse surging underneath the skin at her throat.

She tried to speak but the accuracy of his prediction had frozen her tongue.

'Since my face is still dry, I'll take it Psychic Rafa is accurate on all accounts?'

His arrogance finally loosened her tongue. 'Don't flatter yourself. I told you when you started playing these games that I wouldn't participate. I know you're challenged by any woman who doesn't fall for your charms, but not everyone subscribes to the OMG-Rafael de Cervantes-makes-my-knickers-wet Fan Club.'

Rafael's smile was blinding, but it held a speculation that made her hackles rise. '*Pequeña*, since there's only one way to *test* that you're not a member, I now have something to look forward to. And just like that, my days suddenly seem brighter.'

Heat punched its way through her pelvis but, before Raven could answer, a deep throat cleared behind them.

Marco de Cervantes was as tall as his brother and just as visually stunning to look at but he wore his good looks with a smouldering grace where Rafael wholeheartedly embraced his irreverent playboy status.

Marco nodded to Raven, and glanced at his brother.

'I need to talk to you. You don't mind if I borrow him for five minutes, do you, Raven?'

Relief spiked, headier than the champagne she'd barely drunk. 'Not at all. We weren't discussing anything important.'

Rafael's eyes narrowed at the thin insult, his icy blue eyes promising retribution just before they cleared into their usual deceptively indolent look.

Lifting her glass in a mocking salute, she walked away, piercingly aware that he tracked her every step. Out of his intoxicating, domineering sphere, she heaved in a breath of pure relief and pasted a smile on her face as Sasha beckoned her.

Rafael turned to his brother, mild irritation prickling his skin. 'What's on your mind?' He discarded his champagne and wished he had something stronger.

'You need another hobby besides trying to rile your physiotherapist.'

His irritation grew as Raven disappeared from sight, pulled towards a group of guests by Sasha. 'What's it to you? And why the hell does everyone feel the need to poke their nose into my business?'

Marco shrugged away the question. 'Consider the matter dropped. The old man's been asking for you.' Grey eyes bored sharply into his. 'I think it's time.'

Every bone in his body turned excruciatingly rigid. 'That's for me to decide, surely?' And if he didn't feel he was ready to ask for forgiveness, who was anybody to decide otherwise?

'There's been enough hurt all around, Rafa. It's time to move things forward.'

He spiked tense fingers through his hair. 'You wouldn't be trying to save me again by any chance, would you, brother?'

An impatient look passed through Marco's eyes. 'From the look of things, you don't need saving. Besides, I cut the apron strings when I realised you were driving me so nuts that I was in danger of strangling you with them.'

Rafael beckoned the waiter over and exchanged his untouched champagne for a crystal tumbler of Patrón. 'In that case, we're copacetic. Was there anything else?'

Marco's gaze stayed on him for several seconds before he nodded. 'You sent for the papers for the X1 All-Star event coming up?'

Rafael downed the drink, welcoming the warmth that coursed through his chest. 'Unless I'm mistaken, I'm still the CEO of X1 Premier Management. The events start in three weeks. You delegated some of the event's organisation but it's time for me to take the reins again.'

His brother's gaze probed, worry lurking within. 'Are you sure you don't want to sit this one out—?'

'I'm sure. Don't second-guess me, *mi hermano*. I understand that my racing career may be in question—' He stopped as a chill surged through his veins, obliterating the warmth of moments before. Although he didn't remember his accident, he'd seen pictures of the wreckage in vivid detail. He was very much aware that *lucky to be alive* didn't begin to describe his condition. 'The racing side of my career may be up for debate,' he repeated, beating back the wave of desolation that swelled up inside his chest, 'but my brain still functions perfectly. As for my body…' He looked over as a flash of orange caught his eye. The resulting kick gave him a surge of satisfaction. 'My body will be in top condition before very long.'

Marco nodded. 'I'm happy to hear it. According to Raven, you're on the road to complete recovery.'

'Really?' Rafael made a mental note to have a short, precise conversation with his physio about sharing confidential information.

'…*Dios*, are you listening to me? Never mind, I think it'll be safer for me not to know which part of your anatomy you're thinking with right at this moment. *Bueno*, I'll be in touch later in the week to discuss other business.'

'No need to wait till next week. I can tell you now that I'm back. I own fifty per cent of our business, after all. No reason why you should continue to shoulder my responsibilities.

Come to think of it, you should take a vacation with your family, let me handle things for a while.' He glanced over to where Sasha stood chatting to Raven. As if sensing their attention, both women turned towards them. Marco's face dissolved in a look so cheesy, Rafael barely stopped himself from making retching noises.

'Are you sure?' Marco asked without taking his eyes off his wife. 'Sasha's been on my back about taking some time off. It would be great to take the yacht to the island for a bit.' They joint owned a three-mile island paradise in the Bahamas, a place neither of them had visited in a very long time.

'Great. Do it. I'll handle things here,' Rafael responded.

His brother looked sceptical.

'This is a one-time offer, set to expire in ten seconds,' he pressed as his sister-in-law and his physiotherapist started walking towards them. For the first time he noticed Raven's open-toed high heels and saw the way they made her long legs go on for ever. Sasha said something to her. Her responding smile made his throat dry.

Hell, he had it bad if he was behaving like a hormonal teenager around a woman who clearly had *man issues*.

He barely felt it when Marco slapped his shoulder. 'I'll set things in motion first thing in the morning. I owe you one, brother.'

Rafael nodded, relieved that the disturbing subject of his father had been dropped.

'What are you looking so pleased about?' Sasha asked her husband as they drew level with them.

'I have news that's guaranteed to make you adore me even more than you already do.' He kissed her soundly on the lips before leading her away.

Rafael saw Raven looking after them. 'I do believe if they had a *like* button attached to their backs you would be pressing it right about now?'

Her outraged gasp made him curb a smile. He loved to rile her. Rafael didn't hide from the fact that while he was busy riling Raven Blass, he was busy not thinking about what this place did to him, and that gained him a reprieve from the torment of his memories.

She faced him, bristling with irritation and censure. 'Whereas if you had a *like* button I'd personally start a worldwide petition to have it obliterated and replaced with one that said *loathe*.'

He took her elbow and, despite her resistance, he led her to an exquisitely laid out buffet table. 'We'll discuss my various buttons later. Right now you need to eat something before you wither away. I noticed you didn't eat any breakfast this morning.'

She glared at him. 'I had my usual bowl of muesli and fresh fruit.'

'Was that before or after you spent two hours on my beach contorting yourself in unthinkable shapes in the name of exercise?'

'It's called Krav Maga. It works the mind as well as the body.'

He let his gaze rake her from top to toe. 'I don't dispute the effects on the body. But I don't think it's quite working on the mind.'

He stopped another outraged gasp by stuffing a piece of chicken into her mouth. Her only option, other than spitting it out, was to chew, but that didn't stop her glaring fiercely at him.

Rafael was so busy enjoying the way he got under her skin that he didn't hear the low hum of the electric wheelchair until it was too late.

'*Buenos tardes, mi hijo.* I've been looking for you.' The greeting was low and deep. It didn't hold any censure or hatred or flaying judgement. In fact it sounded just exactly as it would were a loving father greeting his beloved son.

But every nerve of Rafael's being screeched with white-hot pain. His fist clenched around his walking stick until the metal dug excruciatingly into his palm. For the life of him, he couldn't let go. He sucked in a breath as his vision blurred. Before the red haze completely dulled his vision, he saw Raven's concerned look as her eyes darted between him and the wheelchair-bound figure.

'Rafael?'

He couldn't find the words to respond to the greeting. Nor could he find the words to stem Raven's escalating concern.

Dios mío, he couldn't even find the courage to turn around. Because how the hell could he explain to Raven that he and he alone was responsible for making his father a quadriplegic?

CHAPTER THREE

'Do you want to talk about it?'

'The *therapy* in your job title pertains only to my body, not my mind. You'll do well to remember that.'

Raven should've heeded the icy warning, should've just kept her hands on the wheel of the luxury SUV and kept driving towards the stunning glass and steel structure that was Rafael's home on the other side of the de Cervantes estate from his brother's villa.

But her senses jumped at the aura of acute pain that had engulfed Rafael the moment he'd turned around to face the old man in the electric wheelchair. The same pain that surrounded him now. Grey lips were pinched into a thin line, his jaw carved from stone and fingers clamped around his walking stick in a white-knuckled grip. Even his breathing had changed. His broad chest rose and fell in an uncharacteristically shallow rhythm that screamed his agitation.

She pulled over next to a tall acacia tree, one of several hundred that lined the long winding driveway and extended into the exquisitely designed landscape beyond. Behind them, the iron gates, manned by twenty-four-hour security, swung shut.

Narrowed eyes focused with laser-like intensity on her. 'What the hell do you think you're doing?'

'I've stopped because we need to talk about what just happened. Your mental health affects your body's recovery just as much as your physiotherapy regime.'

'Healthy mind, healthy body? That's a piss-poor way of trying to extract the hot gossip, Raven *mía*. You'll need to do much better than that. Why don't you just come out and ask for the juicy details?'

She blew a breath, refusing to rise to the bait. 'Would you tell me if I asked you that?'

'No.'

'Rafael—'

Arctic-chilled eyes narrowed even further. 'In case you didn't already guess, that was my father. Our relationship comes under the subject line of *kryptonite—keep the hell out* to any and all parties.'

'So you can dissect my personal life all you want but yours is off limits?'

His smile was just as icy. 'Certain aspects of my personal life are wide open to you. All you have to do is say the word and I'll be happy to educate you in how we can fully explore it.'

'That is not what I meant.'

'You've taken pains to establish boundaries between us since the moment we met. This is one of *my* boundaries. Attempt to breach it at your peril.'

She frowned. 'Or what? You'll fall back on your default setting of sexual innuendo and taunts? Rafael, I'm only trying to help you.'

His hand slashed through the air in a movement so far removed from his normal laid-back indolence her mouth dropped open. 'I do not need your help unless it's the help I've hired you to provide. Right now I want you to shut up and *drive*.' He clipped out the final word in a hard bite that sent a chill down her spine.

After waiting a minute to steady her own shot nerves, she set the SUV back onto the road, aware of his continued shallow breathing and gritted-jaw iciness. Her fingers clenched over the titanium steering wheel and she practised some nerve-calming breaths of her own.

From the very first, Rafael had known which buttons to push. He'd instinctively known that the subject of sex was anathema to her and had therefore honed in on it with the precision of a laser-guided missile.

Seeing his intense reaction to his father—and she'd known immediately the nearly all-grey-haired man in the wheelchair was his father—had hammered home what she'd been surprised to learn this morning at the chapel, and had somewhat confirmed at Marco's villa: that Rafael, as much as he pretended to be shallow and sex pest-y, had a depth he rarely showed to the world.

Was that why she was so driven to pay penance for the way she'd treated him several months ago—because deep down she thought he was worth saving?

Raven shied away from the probing thought and brought the car to a stop at the end of the driveway.

The wide solid glass door that led into the house swung open and Diego, one of the many staff Rafael employed to run his luxurious home, came down the steps to open her door. In silence, she handed him the car keys and turned to find Rafael rounding the bonnet. The sun glinting off the silver paint cast his face into sharp relief. Her breath snagged in her chest at the masculine, tortured beauty of him. She didn't offer to assist him as he climbed the shallow steps into the house.

In the marble-floored hallway, he shrugged off his suit jacket, handed it to Diego and pulled his shirt tails impatiently from his trousers. At the glimpse of tanned golden flesh a pulse of heat shot through her belly. Sucking in a breath, she looked away, focusing on an abstract painting that took up one entire rectangular pillar in the hallway for an infinitesimal second before she glanced his away again, to find him shoving an agitated hand through his hair.

'Do you need—?' she started.

'Unless I'm growing senile, today's Sunday. Did we not agree we'd give the Florence Nightingale routine a rest on Sundays?'

Annoyance rose to mingle with her concern. 'No, *you* came up with that decree. I never agreed to it.'

Handing his walking stick to a still-hovering Diego, he

started to unbutton his shirt. 'It's a great thing I'm the boss then, isn't it?'

Her mouth dried as several inches of stunning flesh assaulted her senses. When her brain started to short-circuit, she pulled her gaze away. 'Undressing in the hallway, Rafael, really?' She tried to inject as much indifference into her tone as possible but was aware her voice had become unhealthily screechy. 'What do you think—that I'm going to run away in virginal outrage?'

His shameless grin didn't hide the strain and tension beneath. 'At twenty-four, I seriously doubt there's anything virginal about you. No, *mi dulzura,* I'm hoping you'll stay and cheer me on through my striptease.'

The sound that emerged from her throat made his grin widen. 'Don't you want to heal completely? That limp will not go away until you work hard to strengthen your core muscles and realign the bones that were damaged during the accident. If you'd just focus on that we can be rid of each other sooner rather than later.'

Although she thought she saw his shoulders stiffen as he turned to give his shirt to Diego, his grin was still in place when he faced her. 'You're under the impression that I want to be shot of you but you couldn't be further from the truth. I want you right here with me every day.'

'So I can be your whipping girl?'

'I've never been a fan of whips, myself. Handcuffs, blindfolds, the odd paddle, certainly…but whips?' He gave a mock shudder. 'No, not my thing.'

His hand went to the top of his trousers. Deft fingers freed his button, followed by the loud, distinct sound of his zip lowering. She froze. Diego didn't bat an eyelid. 'For goodness' sake, what *are* you doing, Rafael?'

He toed off his shoes and socks. 'I thought it was obvious. I'm going for a swim. Care to join me?'

'I…no, thank you.' The way her temperature had shot up, she'd need a cold shower, not the sultry warmth of Rafael's azure infinity pool. 'But we'll need to talk when you're done. I'll come and find you—' She nearly choked when he dropped his trousers and stepped out of them. The way his designer cotton boxer shorts cupped his impressive man package made all oxygen flee from her lungs. Utterly captivated by the man whose sculpted body, even after the accident that had laid him flat for months, was still the best-looking she'd even seen or worked with, Raven could no more stop herself from staring than she could fly to the moon.

His thighs and legs bore scars from his accident, his calves solid powerful muscle that made the physio in her thrilled to be working with such a manly specimen. Dear Lord, even his feet were sexy, and she'd never been one to pay attention to feet unless they were directly related to her profession.

Helplessly, her gaze travelled back up, past his golden, sculpted chest and wide, athletic shoulders to collide with icy blue eyes.

'My, my, if I didn't enjoy it so much I'd be offended to be treated like a piece of meat.'

She snapped back to her senses to see Diego disappearing up the granite banister-less staircase leading to Rafael's vast first floor suite. The click of his walking stick drew attention back to the man in question. One brow was raised in silent query.

'What do you expect if you insist on making an exhibition of yourself?'

One step brought him within touching distance. 'That's the beauty of free will, *querida*. The ability to walk away when a situation displeases you.'

'If I did that every time you attempted to rile me, I'd never get any work done and you'd still be in the pathetic shape I found you in five weeks ago.'

Another step. Raven breathed in and clenched her fists against the warm, wicked scent that assailed her senses.

'You know what drew me to you when you first joined Team Espíritu?' he breathed.

'I'm sure you're going to enlighten me.'

'Your eyes flash with the deepest hypnotic fire when you're all riled up but your body screams *stay away*. Even the most seductive woman can't pull that off as easily as you can. I'm infinitely fascinated to know what happened to make you this way.'

'Personal subjects are off the table. Besides, I thought you had me all worked out?'

His gaze dropped to her lips. She pressed them together to stop their insane tingling. 'I know the general parameters of your inner angst. But I can't help but feel there's another layer, a deeper reason why you want me with every cell in your body but would chop off your hand before you would even bring yourself to touch me in any but a professional way.'

The ice that encased her soul came from so deep, so dark a place that she'd stopped trying to fathom the depths of it. 'Enjoy your swim, Rafael. I'll come by later to discuss the next steps of your regime.'

'Of course, Mistress Raven. I look forward to the many and varied ways you intend to *whip* me into shape.' With a step sideways that still managed to encroach on her body space and bring even more of his pulsing body heat slapping against her, he adjusted the walking stick and sauntered away in a slow, languid walk.

Hell, even a limping Rafael de Cervantes managed to move with a swagger that made her heart race. Tearing her traitorous gaze away from his tight butt, she hurried up the floating staircase to her room. Gritting her teeth against the firestorm of emotions that threatened to batter her to pieces, she changed into her workout gear. The simple act of donning the familiar attire calmed her jangling nerves.

But she couldn't forget that, once again, Rafael had cut through the outer layer of her defences and almost struck bone, almost peeled back layers she didn't want uncovered.

She pushed the niggling sensation away and shoved her feet into comfortable trainers. After a minute's debate, she

decided on the gym instead of her preferred outdoor regime.
Even though the day was edging towards evening, the Spanish sun blazed far too hot for the gruelling exercise she needed
to restore balance to her equilibrium.

She took the specially installed lift that divided her suite
from Rafael's to the sub-basement level where the state-of-
the-art gym was located. It was the only room in the whole
house that didn't have an exhibitionist's view to the outside.

Rafael's house held no concrete walls, only thick glass in-
terspersed with steel and chrome pillars. At first the feeling of
exposure had preyed on her nerves, but now the beauty of the
architecturally stunning design had won her over. Nevertheless, right this minute she was grateful for the enclosed space
of the gym. Here she didn't need to compose herself, didn't
need to hold back her punches as she slammed her gloved fist
into the punching bag. Pain repeatedly shot up her arms, and
gradually cleared her mind.

She was here to do her job. Which started and ended with
helping Rafael heal properly and regain the utmost mobility. Once she achieved her aim and made peace with her part
in his accident, she could walk away from the crazy, bone-
deep, completely insane attraction she felt for the man who
was in every shape and form the epitome of the man who'd
fathered her.

The man whose playboy lifestyle had mattered to him on
so deep a level he'd turned his back on his parental responsibilities until they'd been forced on him by the authorities.
The same man who'd stood by and barely blinked while his
friends had tried to put their hands on her.

Punch!

Her hand slipped. The bag continued its lethal trajectory
towards her. Only her ingrained training made her sidestep
the heavy-moving bag before it knocked her off her feet. Chest
heaving, she tugged off the gloves and went to the climbing
frame and chalked her hands.

Clamping her lids shut, she regulated her breathing and forced herself to focus.

Rafael would not derail her. She'd made a colossal mistake and vocalised her roiling disgust for his lifestyle at the most inappropriate moment. Whatever the papers had said, Raven knew deep down she was partly, if not wholly, responsible for putting Rafael in the dangerous frame of mind that had caused his accident. She also knew things could've turned out a million times worse than they had. This was her penance. She would help him get back on his feet. Then she would leave and get on with the rest of her life.

Reaching high, she grabbed the first handhold.

By the time she reached the top seven minutes later, her new course of action was clearly formulated.

'I've laid out the itinerary for the next three months. If you cooperate, I'm confident I can get you back to full health and one hundred per cent mobility with little or no after-effects,' she started crisply as she opened the door and entered Rafael's study. She approached his desk, only to stop when she noticed his attention was caught on the papers strewn on his glass-topped desk.

'I'm talking to you, Rafael.'

'I heard you,' he muttered, and held out his hand for the sheet without looking up. After a cursory glance, he started to shake his head. 'This isn't going to work.' He slapped it down and picked up his own papers.

Raven waited a beat. When he didn't look up, she fought a sharp retort. 'May I ask why not?'

'I have several events to host and meetings to attend between now and when the X1 season starts. Your itinerary requires that I stand still.'

She frowned. 'No, it doesn't.'

'It might as well. You've upped the regime from two to three times a day with sports massages thrown in there that would require me to be stationary. And was that *acupuncture*

I saw in there?' His derisive tone made her hackles rise higher. 'I'll be travelling a lot in the next three months. You're sorely mistaken if you think I intend to take time off to sit around being pricked and prodded.'

She watched the light glint off his damp hair. 'What do you mean, you'll be travelling a lot? You're supposed to be recuperating.'

Steely blue eyes met hers and instantly Raven was reminded of the unwavering determination that had seen him win several racing championships since he'd turned professional at nineteen.

'I have a multi-billion-dollar company to run, or have you forgotten?'

'No, I haven't. But wasn't...isn't Marco in charge for the time being? He told me he had everything in hand when we discussed my helping you—'

His eyes narrowed. 'What else did you discuss with my brother?'

Mouth dry, she withstood his stare. 'What do you mean?'

'I expected an element of confidentiality when I hired you...'

'What *exactly* are you accusing me of?'

'You will not discuss details of my health with anyone else but me, is that clear?'

'I didn't—'

'You're glowing.' His gaze raked her face down to her neck and back up again.

'Excuse me?'

'You look...flushed. If I weren't painfully aware of the unlikelihood of it, I'd have said you had just tumbled from a horizontal marathon in a lover's bed. Not quite tumbled to within an inch of your life, more like—'

'Can we get back to this, please?' She waved the sheet in his face then slammed it back in front of him.

He shrugged and sat back in his plush leather chair, the cool, calm businessman back in place. 'Marco has his own company to run…and a new family to attend to. Besides, he's taking a well-earned break, so I'm managing his company as well.'

A wave of shock nearly rendered her speechless. 'And you didn't think to speak to me before you decided all this?'

'I wasn't aware I needed your permission to live my life or run my business.' His voice, a stiletto-thin blade, skimmed close to her skin.

She took a breath and searched for calm, a state which she'd concluded long ago was near on impossible when in Rafael's presence. 'It's part of the contract we agreed. If you're going to take on any substantial amount of work I'll need to know so I can formulate your therapy accordingly. For goodness' sake, you can't go from zero to full-time work in the space of an afternoon. And I really don't know what you were thinking, telling your brother you'd take on this amount of work for the next goodness knows how long!'

Rafael's gaze dropped to her annoyed almost-pout and fought not to continue downward to the agitated heaving of her breasts. Peachy…the smooth skin of her throat glowed a faint golden-pink. He'd long been fascinated by how a woman with jet-black hair such as hers could have skin so pale it was almost translucent. He knew she took care to stay out of the sun and practised her exercises before daybreak.

An image of her, streamlined, sleek and poised upside down in a martial arts pose, slammed into his brain. The groin-hardening effect made him grip his pen harder. His gaze fell once more on her lips and it was all he could do not to round his desk, clasp her face in his hands and taste her. Or maybe coax her round to him, pull down that prim little skirt she'd donned and discover the delights underneath.

Dios, focus!

'Luckily, I don't answer to you, *mi dulzura*.' He certainly had no intention of enlightening her on what he'd been working steadily on for over a month; what he hadn't stopped thinking of since he'd woken from his coma.

Because finding a way to occupy his mind was the only sure way of keeping his many and varied demons at bay.

'...I hope to hell you're not thinking of adding racing to this insane schedule.' She paled a little as she said it and the usual kick of satisfaction surged.

'And what if I am?' He moderated his voice despite the cold fist of pain that lodged in his gut. Unless a miracle happened, his racing career was over. A part of him had accepted that. Deep inside his soul, however, it was another matter.

'I'm hoping it won't come to that. Because you know as well as I do, you're in no shape to get into a racing cockpit.'

He raised an interested brow. 'And how exactly do you intend to stop me?'

Her delectable lips parted but no words emerged, and her eyes took on a haunted look that made him grit his teeth. 'I can't, I suppose. But I think you'll agree you're not in the best shape.'

'Physically or mentally?'

'Only you can judge your mental state but, as your physiotherapist, I'd say you're not ready.'

He finally got his body under enough control to stand. He caught her sharp inhalation when he rounded the desk and perched on the edge next to where she stood. Hazel eyes, wide and spirited, glared at him.

Taking the sheet from her hand, he dropped it on the table, reached across—slowly, so she wouldn't bolt—and traced his forefinger along her jaw. 'Your eyes are so huge right now. You're almost shaking with worry for me. Yet you try and make me think you detest the very ground I walk on.'

Her hand rose to intercept his finger but, instead of pushing it away, she kept a hold of it, imploring eyes boring into his. 'I don't detest you, Rafael. If I did, I wouldn't be here. I'll admit we're...different but—' her shoulders rose and fell under the thin layer of her cotton top '—I'm willing to put aside our differences to help you recuperate properly. And racing before you're ready...come on, you know that's crazy.

Besides, think of your family, of Sasha. Do you think you're being fair to them, putting them through this?'

He froze. 'I've never responded well to emotional blackmail. And leave Sasha out of this. I'll tell you what, if you don't want me to race, you'll have to find other ways to keep me entertained.'

She dropped his hand as if it burned, just like he'd known she would. 'Why does everything always circle back to sex with you?'

'I didn't actually mean that sexually, but what the hell, let's go with it.'

'Stop doing that!'

'Doing what, *mi encantador*?'

'Pretending you're a male bimbo whore.'

'Are you saying I'm not?' He pretended astonishment, the fizz of getting under her skin headier than the most potent wine.

She nodded at the papers on his desk. 'You just reminded me that you run a multi-billion-dollar corporation. I don't care how great you claim to be in bed; you couldn't have made it without using some upstairs skills.'

He leaned back on the table when a twinge of pain shot through his left hip. 'How do you know?'

'You shouldn't sit like that. You're putting too much pressure on your hip.'

Annoyance replaced his buzz. He didn't deny that Raven had made much progress where his previous physios had failed. After all, it was the reason Team Espíritu had hired her as his personal therapist last year. She was the best around and got impressive results with her rigorous regime. But she'd always been able to brush him off as if he were a pesky fly.

He remained in his exact position, raising a daring brow when her gaze collided with his. His blood thickened when she took the dare and stepped closer.

Without warning, her hand shot out and grabbed his hip. Her thumb dug into his hipbone where the pain radiated from.

A few rotations of pressure-based massage and he wanted to moan with relief.

'Why do you fight me when you know I'm the best person to help you get better?' she breathed.

'Because my *mamá* told me I never took the easy way out. You will never get me to ask how high when you say jump.'

She paused for a second, then continued to massage his hip. 'You never talk about your mother,' she murmured.

Tension rippled through him. 'I never talk about anyone in my family. The prying all comes from you, *bonita*. You've made it a mission to upturn every single rock in my life.'

'And yet I don't feel in any way enlightened about your life.'

'Maybe because I'm an empty vessel.' He tried damn hard not to let the acid-like guilt bleed through his voice.

'No, you're not. You just like to pretend you are. Have you considered that by pretending to be something you're not, all you're doing is attracting attention to the very thing you wish to avoid?'

'That's deep. And I presume that thought challenges you endlessly?'

Her hand had moved dangerously close to his fly. If she looked down or moved her actions a few inches west, she'd realise that, despite their verbal sparring skimming the murkier waters of his personal life, he was no less excited by her touch.

In fact, he wasn't ashamed to admit that he found the return of his libido exhilarating. For a few weeks after he'd emerged from his coma it'd been touch and go. His doctors had cautioned him that he might not resume complete sexual function. Raven Blass's appearance in his hospital room five weeks ago had blown that misdiagnosis straight out of the water.

'No,' she responded. 'I know better than to issue challenges to you.'

'You're such a buzzkill,' he said, but he felt relieved that she'd decided to leave the matter of his mother alone.

He saw the faintest trace of a smile on her face before it disappeared. Her fingers moved away, rounded his hip and settled into his back. The movement brought her closer still, her chest mere inches from his. Firm, relief-bringing fingers dug into his muscle. Again he suppressed a moan of relief.

'I know. But think how smug I'd feel if you got back into racing before you were ready and reversed your progress. You'd never hear the end of it if you proved me right.'

The sultry movement of her mouth was a siren call he didn't try very hard to resist. His forefinger was gliding over her mouth before he could stop himself. Her fingers stilled before digging painfully into his back. The rush of her breath over his finger sent his pulse thundering.

'Or I could die. And this relentless song and dance could be over between us. Once and for all.'

CHAPTER FOUR

THE CALM DELIVERY of his words, spoken with barely a flicker of those lush jet eyelashes, froze her to the core.

'Is that what you want? To die?' Her words were no more than a whisper, coated with the shock that held her immobile.

'We all have to die some time.'

'But why, Rafael? Why do you wish to hurry the process when every rational human being fights to stay alive?'

'*Mi tesoro*, rational isn't exactly what most people think when they look at me.'

'That's not an answer.' She realised she was hanging on to him with a death claw but, for the life of her, Raven couldn't let go. She feared her legs would fail her if she did. And hell, she wasn't even sure *why* Rafael's explanation was so important to her. For all she knew, it was another statement meant to titillate and shock. But, looking closer, her blood grew colder. Something in his expression wasn't quite right. Or, rather, it was too right, as if he held his statement with some conviction. 'What is it, Rafael? Please tell me why you said that.'

'Quid pro quo, sweetheart. If I bare my soul, will you bear yours?'

'Would that give you something to live for?'

Raven could've sworn she heard the snap of his jaw as he went rigid in her arms. Grasping her by the elbows, he set her away from him and straightened to his impressive six foot three inches. His lids shuttered his expression and he returned to the seat behind his desk.

'The amateur head-shrinking session is over, *chiquita*. Modify your regime to accommodate travel and liaise with Diego if you'll need special equipment for where we'll be travelling. We leave on Wednesday.' He reeled off their intended destinations before picking up a glossy photo of the latest Cervantes sports car.

Knowing she wouldn't make any more headway with him, she turned to leave.

'Oh, and Raven?'

'Yes?'

'We'll be attending several high profile events, so make sure you pack something other than kick-boxing shorts, trainers and tank tops. As delectable as they are, they won't suit.'

Raven fought the need to smash her fist into the nearest priceless vase as she left Rafael's study. Not because he would see her, although the glass walls meant he would, but because *not* losing control was paramount if she wished to maintain her equilibrium.

She'd fought long and hard to channel her tumultuous emotions into useful energy when, at sixteen, she'd realised how very little her father cared for her. For far too long, she'd been so angry with the world for taking her mother away and replacing her with a useless, despicable parent, she'd let her temper get the better of her.

Rafael could do his worst. She would not let him needle her further.

Taking the sheet into the vast living room, she spent the next hour revising Rafael's regime and speaking to Diego about organising the equipment she would need. Again she felt unease and a healthy amount of frustrated anger at Rafael's decision to return to X1 racing. She didn't shy away from the blunt truth that she herself wanted to avoid the inevitable return.

Even though she'd been paid handsomely by Team Espíritu and treated well by the team, she'd always felt ill at ease in that world. She didn't have to dig deep to recognise the reason.

Sexual promiscuity had been almost a given in the paddock. Hell, some even considered it a challenge to sleep with as many bodies as possible during one race season.

She'd received more than her fair share of unwanted male attention and, by the end of her first season, she'd known she was in danger of earning a *frigid* badge. Ironically, it was Sasha Fleming's catapult into the limelight as the team's lead racer that had lessened male interest in her. For the first time, female paddock professionals were seen as more than just the next notch on a bedpost.

'A two-line frown. I don't know whether to be pleased or disappointed.'

She looked up to find Rafael standing a few feet away, two drinks in his hand and his walking stick dangling from his arm. He held one out to her and she accepted and thanked him for the cold lime based cocktail she'd grown to love since coming to Leon.

'I was thinking about how it would be to return to the X1 circuit.'

'Shouldn't that warrant a three-line frown since I feature in there somewhere?'

'Wow, are you really that self-centred? A psychologist would have a field day with you, you know that?'

With a very confident, very careless shrug, he sank into the seat next to her. 'They'd have to fight off hordes of adoring fans first. Not to mention you.'

'Me? Why would I mind?'

'You're very possessive about me. If you had your way, I'd stay right here, doing your every bidding and following you around like a besotted puppy.'

Eternally thankful she'd swallowed her first sip, Raven stared open-mouthed. Several seconds passed before she could close her mouth. 'I'm stunned speechless.'

'Enough for me to sneak a kiss on you?'

Blood rushed to her head and much lower, between her legs, a throbbing started that should've shamed her. Instead, she exhaled and decided to give herself a break. A girl could only withstand so many shocks in one day.

'Earth to Raven. I don't know how to interpret a wish for a kiss when you go into a trance at the thought of one.'

'I…what?'

'I said kiss me.'

'No. I don't think that's a good idea.'

'It's a great idea. Look at me; I can barely walk. *You'd* be taking advantage of *me*.' His smile held a harsh edge that made the Rafael de Cervantes charm even more lethal.

'Whatever. It's not going to happen. Now, is there anything else I can help you with?'

His sigh was heavy and exaggerated. 'Bianca is almost ready to serve dinner. I figure we have twenty minutes to burn. Shall we be very English and talk about the weather before then?'

'The weather is fantastic. Now, let's talk about your return to X1. I don't wish to get personal…'

His low laugh made heat rush into her face.

'What I mean is…you'll have to be careful when it comes to being…um…'

'Just spit it out, Raven.'

'Fine. Sex. You can't have sex.'

He clutched his chest, then tapped carefully on his sculpted muscle. '*Dios*, I think my heart just stopped. You can't *say* things like that.'

'I mean it. The last thing you need to be doing is chasing after paddock bunnies. You could reverse any progress we've made in the last few weeks. Your pelvis needs time to heal properly. You do want to get better, don't you?'

'Yes, but at what cost? My libido could just shrivel away and die,' he returned without the barest hint of shame while she…she'd grown so hot she had to take a hasty sip of her drink.

'It won't.' She set her glass down on the table. 'Not unless you put too much stress on your body by taking on too much. Look, I'm not asking for much. I'm saying keep your…keep it in your pants for just a little bit longer, until you're more fully recovered.'

He opened his mouth but she raised her hand before he could speak. 'And please don't say you need sex to recover. Despite what you want everyone to think, you're not a sex addict. In fact you were one of the most disciplined men I knew when it came to dedication to racing. All I'm saying is apply that same discipline to your…needs, at least for the time being.'

Sensual masculine lips tilted at the corners. 'I think there was a compliment in there somewhere. Fine, I'll take your lecture under advisement.'

'You need to do more than that, Rafael. Your injuries are too serious to take recovery lightly.'

He shoved a hand through his hair. '*Dios*, did I call you a buzzkill earlier?'

'I believe you did.'

'Congratulations, you've just been upgraded to manhood-killer. Ah, here comes Bianca. Let's hope she's got something to revive me after that complete emasculation.'

'Yeah, my heart bleeds.'

Rafael tried to follow what the financial newsreader was saying on the large high definition screen on his plane. He failed.

Opposite him, ensconced in the club chair, Raven twirled a pen between her lips as she read and made notes on a piece of paper. On any other woman he'd have ridiculed such a blatant sexual ploy. But he knew the woman opposite him was unaware of what she was doing. And its totally groin-hardening effect on him.

Giving up on finding out how the Dow-Jones was doing, he turned off the TV and settled back in his seat.

She raised her head and looked at him with those stunning hazel eyes. 'What?'

'How did you get into physiotherapy?'

She regarded him for several seconds before she depressed the top of her pen. 'The random kindness of strangers.'

He raised an eyebrow.

She shrugged. 'A chance meeting with an ex-PE teacher in my local park when I was seventeen changed my life.'

'Was he hot?'

She rolled her eyes. '*She* realised I loved to exercise but I had no interest in being an athlete. We met and talked a few times. About a month later she took me to the local sports centre where professional athletes trained and introduced me to their head coach. By the end of the day I knew what I wanted to be.'

'And she did this all out of the goodness of her heart?'

'She realised I had…anger issues and worked to give me focus. She didn't have to, so yes, I guess she did.'

He held back the need to enlighten her that nothing in life came free; that every deed held a steep price. 'What were you angry about?' he asked instead.

'Life. My lot. What do most teenagers get angry about at that age?'

'I don't know. I was on the brink of realising my dream and getting ready to step into my very first X1 racing car when I seventeen. I was pretty happy with life at that age.' Blissfully ignorant of the consequences fate had in store for him.

'Of course you were. Well, some of us weren't that lucky.'

'Not all luck is good. Some comes from the devil himself, *bonita*. So, you achieved your light bulb moment, then what?'

Her gaze slid from his. He forced himself to remain quiet.

'Although my teacher helped direct my vision, I couldn't really do anything about it. Not at seventeen. I spent most of that year counting the days until my eighteenth birthday.'

'Why?'

He saw her reticence. Wondered why he was probing when he never intended to get as personal himself.

After a minute, she answered. 'Because turning eighteen meant I could make my own decisions, get myself away from…situations I didn't like.'

Rafael knew she wouldn't elaborate more than that. He respected that but it didn't stop him from speculating. And the directions his thoughts led him made his fist tighten on his armchair.

Raven's attitude towards sex and to him in particular had always puzzled him, not because of the women who had fallen over their feet to get to him since he'd shot up and grown broader shoulders at sixteen.

No, what had always intrigued him was the naked attraction he saw in her eyes, coupled with the fortress she put in place to ensure that attraction never got acted upon.

It didn't take a genius to know something had happened to make her that way. Her little morsel of information pointed to something in her childhood. He tensed, suddenly deciding to hell with respecting her boundaries.

'What happened to you? Were you abused?' he rasped, his fingernails digging into the armrest.

She froze. Darkened eyes shot to his before she glanced out of the porthole. When she returned her gaze to his, the haunted look had receded but not altogether disappeared. 'Have you ever heard of the term—the gift of the gab?'

He nodded.

'Well, my father could make the world's most famous orators look like amateurs. His silver tongue could charm an atom into splitting, so the term *abuse* never could stick, especially if the social worker who dealt with any allegation happened to be a woman. So technically, no, I wasn't abused.'

His teeth gritted so hard his jaw ached. Inhaling deeply, he forced himself to relax. 'What the hell did he do to you?'

She blinked, looked around as if realising where they were, or rather *who* she was with. Her features closed into neutral and she snapped the pen back out. Lowering her gaze, she snatched up her papers from her lap and tapped them into a neat sheaf. 'It doesn't matter. I'm no longer in that situation.'

Rafael almost laughed. Almost told her being out of the situation didn't mean she was out of its control. The past had tentacles that stretched to infinity. He was in the prime place to know.

His father...his mother. Not a day went by that the memories didn't burn behind his retinas—a permanent reminder only death would wipe away. They plagued him in his wakeful hours and followed him into his nightmares. He could never get away from what he'd done to them. No matter how far he went, how much he drank or how many women he let use his body.

'I've revised the regime.' Raven interrupted his thoughts, her tone crisp, businesslike. Her lightly glossed lips were set in a firm line and her whole demeanour shrieked step back in a way that made him want to reach across and *ruffle* her.

Grateful for something else to focus on rather than his dark past, he settled deeper into his seat and just watched her.

She flicked a glance at him and returned her gaze to the papers. 'I've ensured that we'll have a clear hour every morning for a thorough physio session. You already know that if you sit or stand for extended periods of time your body will seize up so I'll recommend some simple exercises for when you're in meetings, although the ideal situation would be for you not to *be* in meetings for extended periods.'

'I'll see about scheduling video conferences for some of the meetings.'

Her head snapped up, surprise reflected in her gaze. 'You will?'

'Don't sound so surprised. My boundless vanity draws the line at cutting my nose off to spite my face. You should know that by now.'

'If you can video conference, then why do you need to be there in the first place?'

'Like any other organisation, there's always a hotshot usurper waiting in the wings, ready to push you off into the great abyss at the slightest hint of weakness. I've grown attached to my pedestal.'

'You speak as if you're decrepit.'

'I haven't had sex in months. I *feel* decrepit. And with your decree of no sex, I feel as if my life has no purpose.'

'You mean you miss your fans and just want to resume basking in their admiration?'

'I'm a simple man, Raven. I love feeling wanted.'

Her lips compressed again, although he saw the shadows had faded from beneath her eyes and her colour had returned to her cheeks. He barely stopped himself from feeling inordinately pleased by the achievement.

She stared down again at the sheet in her hand. 'Why Monaco?'

'Why not? It's the glamour capital of motor racing. Most of the current and ex-drivers live there. It affords the best platform for the launch of the All-Star event.'

'Will there be any actual racing?' she asked.

He caught the wariness in her tone and suppressed another smile. Like it or not, Raven Blass was worried about him.

Just like Marco. Just like Sasha… Just like his father. He had no right to that level of concern from them. From anyone.

The tiny fizz of pleasure disappeared.

'There won't be any actual racing until we get to Monza in two weeks' time.' His brisk tone made her eyes widen. Rafael didn't bother to hide his annoyance. 'Racing is my life, Raven. I haven't decided whether or not I'll ever get behind another steering wheel but that decision will be mine to make and mine alone. So stop the mental hand-wringing and concentrate on making me fit again, *si*?'

The large, luxurious private jet banked left and Raven felt her heart lurch with it. Below them, the dazzling vista of the Côte d'Azure glittered in the late winter sunshine. With little over a month before the racing season started, the drivers would be in various stages of pre-season tests in Barcelona.

Which was where Rafael would've been had he not had his accident.

At nearly thirty-one, he'd been in his prime as a racing driver and had commanded respect and admiration all over the world. He still did if the million plus followers he commanded on social media and adoring fans from the racing paddock were anything to go by. But Raven hadn't considered how he must be feeling to be out of the racing circuit for the coming year. And what it would do to him if he could never race again.

'I'm sorry. I didn't mean to make this any harder for you than it already is,' she murmured.

She braced herself for his usual innuendo-laden comeback.

'*Gracias*,' was all he came out with instead. 'I appreciate that.'

Before she could respond, a stewardess emerged from behind a curtain to announce they would be landing in minutes.

'Time for the crazy circus to begin. You ready?' He raised a brow at her.

'Sure. After living with you for five weeks, Rafael, I think I'm ready for anything.'

His deep laugh tugged at a place inside her she'd carefully hidden but he seemed to lay bare with very little effort.

'Let's hope you don't end up eating those words, *querida*.'

'I probably will, but…promise me one thing?'

He stilled and his eyes gleamed dangerously at her from across the marble-topped table between them. Finally he nodded.

'Promise me you'll let me know if it all gets too much. No glib or gloss. I can't do my job properly if you don't tell me what's going on.'

His eyes narrowed. 'This job, it's that important to you?'

'Yes, it is. I…I'm here to make amends. I can't ever take back what I said to you, and you don't remember if what I said played a part in your accident. Your recovery is important to me, yes.'

'Hasn't anyone told you being in a hurry to fall on your sword is an invitation to a shameless opportunist like me?'

'Rafael—'

He made a dismissive gesture. 'You won't need me to report my well-being to you, *querida*. You'll be with me twenty-four seven.'

The plane, lending perfect punctuation to his words, chose that moment to touch down. Rafael was up and heading towards the doors before the jet was fully stationary.

Jumping up, she hurried after him.

And realised—once a thousand flashlights exploded in her face on exit—that he hadn't been joking when he'd referred to the circus.

Monaco in late winter was just as glorious as it was during the summer race weekend but with an added bonus of considerably fewer people. But for the paparazzi dogging their every move, Raven could've convinced herself she was on holiday.

After a series of introductions and short but numerous meetings, they were finally driven higher and higher into the mountains above Monte Carlo. Glancing out at the spectacular view spread beneath them, her senses came alive at the beauty around her. It was different to the rugged gorgeousness of Rafael's estate in León, but breathtaking nonetheless.

'Don't you usually stay at the Hôtel de France?' She referred to the exquisite five-star hotel where all his meetings had taken place with the upper echelons of his X1 Premier Management team.

'I prefer to stay there during the race season. But not this time.'

She wondered at the cryptic remark until they arrived at their destination. Wrought iron gates swung wide to reveal a jaw-droppingly stunning art deco villa. The design wasn't unique to the French Riviera but several marked add-ons—large windows and a hint of steel and chrome here and there—made it stand out from the usual.

'Who lives here?' she asked.

'For the next few days, you and me and the usual number of complementary staff. It used to belong to an Austrian countess. I'm toying with the idea of buying it, making this my permanent base.'

She faced him in surprise. 'You're considering leaving León?'

He shrugged, seeming carefree, but his expression was shuttered. 'I haven't really lived full time in León for a very long time. It won't be a big deal.'

'Have you discussed it with Marco and Sasha? Won't they mind?'

'They'd be relieved not to have an invalid cluttering up the place, I expect.'

She suspected his brother and wife thought nothing of the sort but chose not to express that opinion. 'But…it's your home. Won't you miss it?'

'It's only bricks and mortar, *bonita.*'

Realising he meant it, she frowned. '*Is* there a place you actually call home?'

Raven was unprepared for the darkness that swept over his features. In a blink of an eye it was gone, his face restored to its rugged, breathtaking handsomeness that set so many female hearts aflutter whenever the spectacular Rafael de Cervantes made an appearance.

'Rafael?' she probed when he remained silent.

'A long time ago, I did. But, like everything else in my life, I trashed it completely and utterly. Now—' he pushed the door of the limo open, stepped out and held out a hand for her '—come in and tell me what you think. I read somewhere that a woman's opinion is priceless when choosing a house, especially a woman you're not sleeping with. Personally, I disagree with that assertion but I've been known to be wrong once or twice.'

She managed to hold her tongue until the trio of staff who greeted them at the door had taken up their luggage. The minute they were alone, she faced Rafael in the large open style living room, which had an exquisitely moulded ceiling that extended over two floors. Once again—and she was beginning to notice a pattern—the room consisted mostly of windows, although this villa had a few solid walls.

'What did you mean when you said you've trashed everything in your life?' she asked.

He flung his walking stick into the nearest chair and made his way slowly towards her. Stopping a mere foot away, he glanced down at her.

'I was hoping you'd forgotten that.'

'I haven't, and I don't really think you meant me to.'

His smile was fleeting, poignant, and barely touched his eyes. 'I guess my probing on the plane makes you feel you're entitled to a certain…reciprocity?'

'No, I don't. I shared a little of my past with you because I wanted to. You don't have to feel obliged to return the favour but I'd like to know all the same.'

'Tell me what you think of the villa first.'

Her gaze took in the various OTT abstract art and cutting edge sculptures and high-spec lighting and shrugged. Every item in the room shrieked opulence a little too loudly. 'I like it but I don't love it. I think it's trying too hard to be something it's not. I don't think it suits you.'

He glanced around at the plush leather chairs and carefully placed art and sculptures, the high-tech gadgets and priceless rugs.

'Hmm, you could be right. Although that single armchair looks perfect for…de-stressing.'

'Answer my question, Rafael. Why don't you have a home any more?'

His smile dimmed slowly until only raw, untrammelled pain reflected in his eyes. He held his breath for a long, interminable moment, then he slowly exhaled. 'Because, *querida*, everything that meant a damn to me went up in a ball of flames eight years ago.'

CHAPTER FIVE

THE GLITTERING BALLROOM of the Hôtel de France had been re-designed to look like a car showroom, albeit a very expensive car showroom, complete with elaborately elegant priceless chandeliers.

A vintage Bentley MkVI Donington Special from Rafael's own car collection gleamed beneath a spotlight in the centre of the room.

Raven stood to one side as guests continued to stream in from the Automobile Club de Monaco where the X1 All-Star event had kicked off with an opening by the resident head of the Monégasque royal family.

Glancing at the door, she caught sight of Rafael as he chatted to the head of one of the largest car manufacturers in the world. Dressed in a black tuxedo with the customary studded shirt and bow tie, it was the most formal she'd seen him. The sheer stomach-clenching magnetism he exuded made her clutch her champagne flute harder to stem the fierce reaction that threatened to rock her off her feet.

As she watched he laughed in response to a joke. Looking at him, it was hard to believe he was the same man who, for a minuscule moment in time, had bared a part of his soul to her at the villa three days ago. The moment had been fleeting—as most of those moments were with Rafael. Hell, he hadn't even bothered to elaborate after that one cryptic statement about the ball of flames. But his pain had been unmistakable, visceral in a way that had cut through her defences.

Far from recoiling from the man he'd revealed, she'd wanted to draw closer, ease his pain.

I'm going loopy.

He glanced over suddenly and held up three fingers. Her

fingers flew up her face to touch her forehead before she could stop herself. Feeling a wave of heat creep up at his knowing smile, she flung a vaguely rude sign his way and turned her back on him.

He found her minutes later. 'Are you avoiding me?'

'Nope. You seem to be in your element. How's your hip?'

'Not well enough to attempt a paso doble but I'm holding my own.'

'You never told me what all of this is in aid of.'

'Have you never been to an All-Star event?' he asked.

She shook her head. 'I don't tend to involve myself in out of season activities. I've heard of it, but only in vague terms.'

'So what *do* you do when the season ends?' He latched onto the revelation.

Raven bit the inside of her lip, then decided she had nothing to lose by revealing just a little bit more about her personal life. 'I work with injured soldiers, mostly from Afghanistan and Iraq.'

His eyes narrowed slightly, a solemn look descending over his face. 'This must seem so very pointless and horribly ostentatious to you in comparison.'

'Since I don't know exactly what *this* is, I'm prepared to reserve judgement.'

'*This* is nothing but a huge elaborate scheme to get rich people to preen and back-slap while reaching into their pockets to fund a few charities.'

'Good heavens, in that case I condemn you all to Hades,' she said around the smile she couldn't seem to stop.

'Some of us would feel at home there,' he murmured. The bleakness in his voice made her glance up at him but his features gave nothing away.

Deciding to let it go, she glanced around the glittering ballroom. 'It must be nice to click your fingers and have everything fall into place for you like this.'

'Not quite…everything.' His gaze dropped to her lips before returning to capture hers.

Her pulse kicked hard. She fought to pull her gaze away from his but it only went as far as his mouth. 'Well…consider yourself fortunate, gluttony being a sin and all that.' She attempted another smile. When Rafael's own mouth curved into a smile, her heart did a hugely silly dance then proceeded to bash itself against her ribcage.

He beckoned a waiter, took Raven's champagne and exchanged it for a fresher-looking glass. He stopped her with a restraining hand on her arm when she went to sip it.

'Take it easy. It may look like champagne but it's not.'

She eyed the drink warily. 'What is it?'

'It's called Delirium. Don't worry, it's not as sinister or as sleazy as it sounds. Sip it slowly, tell me what you think.'

She did and nearly choked on the tart, potent taste. Almost immediately, the tartness disappeared to leave her tongue tingling with a thousand sensations that made her eyes widen. 'Oh my goodness, it's incredible. What's in it?'

'Edible gold dust and the tiniest drop of adrenaline.'

'You're kidding!'

'About the adrenaline, *sí*, but not the gold dust. Although, in my opinion, it's wasted in the drink. I can think of much better uses for it.' Again his words held a note quite different from his usual innuendo-laden tone.

The ground didn't quite shift but Raven felt a distinct rumble and decided to proceed with caution. 'You were about to tell me about the All-Star event.'

'It's an event I hold every year to get all the racing drivers across various racing formulas together before the season starts. Here we can be just friends, instead of championship competitors, while raising money. It's also an opportunity for retired motor racers to still feel part of the sport for as long as they want to.'

'How many events are there in total?'

'Six races in six countries.' He waved to a grey-haired man who stood with a towering brunette with the hugest diamond ring Raven had ever seen adorning her finger. When the couple beckoned them over, Rafael sighed and took her elbow.

Raven's irritation at having to share Rafael was absurd considering he was the host. But, short of being rude, she had no choice but to let herself be led to the couple.

'Rafael!' the brunette's husky voice gushed a second before she threw herself into Rafael's arms. Dropping Raven's arm, he deftly caught the woman before she could unbalance him and laughed off her throaty murmurs of apology.

They conversed in fluent French as Raven stood to the side.

'Let me introduce you—Sergey Ivanov and his wife, Chantilly. Sergey owns the Black Rock team.'

'And I own his heart,' Chantilly gushed. But even while she planted an open-mouthed kiss on her husband, her eyes were gobbling up Rafael.

Raven tried not to retch as she murmured what she hoped were appropriate conversational responses. After ten unbearable minutes, she was about to make her excuses and escape to the ladies' room when she saw Chantilly reach into her bag. With her husband deep in conversation with Rafael, neither man noticed as she withdrew an expensive lipstick and pulled closer to Rafael.

Raven barely held back her horrified gasp as she saw what Chantilly was doing.

'Did she write her number on your walking stick?' she asked the moment the couple walked away.

He lifted the stick and peered at it. 'Hmm, I believe she did. Interesting…'

Irrational anger bubbled up through her. 'Excuse me.' She barely spat out the words before marching off to the ladies' room. She forced calming breaths into her lungs, calling on every control-restoring technique she knew to help her regain her equanimity.

But when she couldn't even summon up the will to make conversation on the ride back to the villa, she knew she'd failed.

At the door, she bit out a terse goodnight, nearly tripping over the hem of the black sequined gown she'd hastily shopped for in Monaco that morning. She was unused to such elaborate, expensive outfits, as was her credit card, but as she went up to her room, the slide of the seductive material over her heated skin was unmistakable.

Or was it Rafael's gaze on her bare back that caused sensations to skitter all over her body?

She didn't care. All she cared about was getting away from the man who, in more ways than she was willing to admit, was cut from the same cloth as her father.

'I can feel the volcanic waves rising off your body,' Rafael drawled as they finished the last of his exercises next to the large, sparkling infinity pool the next morning. 'I hope your outrage didn't keep you up all night?' His blatant amusement set her teeth on edge.

She stepped back from the bench she'd set up outside, and especially from the man whose potent sweat-mingled scent made her head swim. Taking a deep breath, she fought the feeling.

'Are you seriously so without a moral compass that you don't see anything wrong with a married woman slipping you her phone number right in front of her husband?' she asked, her insides twisting with raw acid.

'Your claws are showing again, *piqueña*.'

'I don't have claws, certainly not where you're concerned. I'm merely disgusted.'

From his position lying flat on the bench, he rose smoothly into a sitting position. 'But you could be so much more if you'd just say the word.'

Flinging a towel onto a nearby chair, she whirled to face him. She tried to tell herself her heart pumped with outrage but underlying that was another emotion she flatly refused to examine. 'For the thousandth time, I'm here to make sure you heal properly, not be your sex pet!'

He rubbed his chin thoughtfully in the morning light, a smile teasing his lips. 'Sex pet. *Dios*, the sound of that makes my pulse race, especially seeing as you're just the right size and shape for a pet.' He shut his eyes, one long arm lifting to trace the air. 'I can just see my hand gliding over that glorious raven hair, sliding down the side of your elegant neck. Of course, you'd gasp in outrage. That's when I'd slide my finger over your full, sexily kissable mouth. And if you were to nip it with just the right amount of pressure—'

She gulped. 'Dammit, Rafael—'

'Shh! Don't spoil my fantasy. The sweat trickling down your chest now just makes me want to undo those no-nonsense buttons and follow it with my tongue.'

Raven glanced down and, sure enough, a bead of sweat was making its way between her breasts. Heat slammed inside her, setting off trails of fire everywhere it touched as if seeking an outlet. This wasn't good. Fires like this eventually escaped, sought the oxygen they needed to burn. Oxygen that looked temptingly, deliciously like the half-naked man in front of her. She could never let it escape, never let it burn because she had a feeling this particular conflagration would be nearly impossible to put out.

She'd more than learned her lesson. She'd been burned badly. Never again.

'Rafael, unless you want to spend the rest of the morning sitting here burning to a crisp, I suggest you zip it and help me get you indoors.'

With a put-upon sigh, he opened his eyes. His low laugh bounced on the morning air before ricocheting through parts of her she didn't want to think about or even acknowledge. 'All right, sex pet. I'll keep my lustful thoughts to myself. But if at any time you want a demonstration, don't hesitate to ask.'

'I won't.'

His smile grew even more wicked, more dangerous than she felt able to cope with. 'You won't hesitate?'

'I won't ask,' she stated firmly, dragging her eyes from the sweat-sheened torso that gleamed mere feet from her.

For several seconds he held her gaze, challenging her with the unabashed heat in his eyes, as if daring her to refuse him.

Raven stood before him, bracing herself and silently praying he would give up or move. Or something!

Finally, he dropped his gaze and reached for his walking stick. With the other hand he pulled her closer and braced his arm over her waist.

'So, you're concerned about my moral compass?' he asked in a droll voice.

'Don't let it go to your head. Sergey seems like a decent man. Are you not concerned about how he'll feel when he finds out you're intending to call his wife for a tryst?'

His laugh was deep and long.

'A *tryst*? That sounds so…decadent.'

She leaned forward, hoping her hair would hide the renewed flush of her cheeks. 'Don't mock me, Rafael. I can still ensure you never walk again.'

'Spoilsport.' He gave a dramatic sigh. 'Before you unleash your many weapons on me, I have no intention of calling or *trysting* with Chantilly. It's a little dance we do. She slips notes and numbers in my pocket. Sergey and I pretend we don't notice.'

She stopped dead. 'You mean he knows?'

His expression was world-weary and full of cynicism. 'He's old enough to be her grandfather, *bonita*. He knows she's not with him for his virility and good looks. Sorry if that bursts your happy little moral bubble.'

The rest of the slow journey to his study was conducted in silence. Raven concentrated hard on ignoring the relief fizzing through her.

She succeeded only because with every step his body bumped against her, his warm, tensile body making her so hyper-aware of her own increased heartbeat. His scent washed over her. She swallowed, the knowledge that it was wrong to feel this way about her patient doing nothing to stop the arrows of lust shooting into her abdomen.

By the time the reached the long sofa that faced the large floor-to-ceiling window in his study, Raven wasn't sure which one of them was breathing heavier.

Rafael slumped into the seat and rested his head on the back of the sofa. Lines of strain bracketed his mouth. Her heart lurched for him.

'Are you okay?'

'Nothing a new hip won't sort out.'

'I can get you some painkillers to ease the pain?'

His jaw clenched. 'No.' From day one, Rafael had refused pain relief, opting for physical therapy to heal his body.

'You have three meetings tomorrow before we leave. I think you should cancel them. Your pelvis isn't as fluid as it could be…and please, no *double entendre*. I mean it. I…I advise you to rethink and let Marco to take over.'

Every last trace of mirth left his face and eyes. His jaw clenched tight and he speared her with suddenly cold eyes. 'I'm not cancelling anything. And my brother and Sasha will be staying exactly where they are.'

The sudden descent into iciness made her shiver. 'Is it true you tried to break them up?' she blurted before she could stop herself.

His gaze grew colder. 'You're straying into none-of-your-business territory, *chiquita*.'

'I thought we were past that? After all, you seem to feel free to stray into my life whenever you feel like it. I'm merely returning the gesture.'

He locked gazes with her for endless seconds. Then he shrugged. 'Okay. Yes, I tried to break them up.'

'Why?'

'Because it seemed like a great idea at the time. Obviously, it didn't work.'

'It wasn't because you loved her?'

Why was she doing this? Asking questions she was fairly certain she didn't want answers to.

'Love? Yes, love. I did it out of love. Twisted, isn't it? If you had a lover too, I'd probably try to separate you from him.'

She frowned. 'Why would you do that?'

He laughed, a half bitter, half amused sound that chilled her nerves. 'Haven't you noticed yet, Raven? I like chaos. I like to cause as much damage as possible wherever I go. Haven't you learned this of me by now? I'm trouble with a capital T.'

She tried for a shrug. 'Some women go for that sort of thing, I hear.'

'But not you, *si*? You remind me of one of the girls I went to Sunday school with.'

Shock held her rigid. 'You went to Sunday school?'

He nodded, the unholy gleam in his eyes lightening the blue depths. 'Religiously. My mother was very keen I got into heaven.'

She laughed at the very idea. She knew no one more devilish in temperament and looks than Rafael de Cervantes.

His grin widened. 'The idea of me in heaven is laughable?'

'In the extreme. You'd corrupt all the other angels within seconds.'

'And they'd love every minute of it.'

'I bet.'

Laughter faded, slowly replaced by an incisive look that should've been her first warning. 'You hide your pain underneath a veneer of blistering efficiency.'

'While you hide yours under the cover of irreverent, sometimes callous charm.'

He reached out a hand for her, and Raven found herself moving towards him, his aura drawing her in like a moth to a flame.

When he patted the seat next to him, she sat down. 'What a pair we are,' he muttered.

She shrugged. 'I guess we must do what we need to do to protect ourselves.'

'From the outside world, yes. But we know what the other is. So there's no need for pretence with us.'

His smile slowly faded to leave a serious, probing look that made her whole body tingle. Slowly he reached out and clasped his hand around her nape. Effortlessly, he drew her forward. She wet her lips before she could stop herself. His groan echoed the deep, dark one inside her.

'What do you want from me, Rafael?' she muttered, her tongue feeling thick in her mouth.

'Nothing you aren't prepared to give me.'

'Don't pretend you won't take more than your fair share.'

His head dropped an inch closer. 'What can I say, I'm a greedy, greedy bastard.'

'What the hell am I doing?'

'Letting go. Living a little. Just because you were hurt before doesn't mean you have to stop living. Pleasure, in the right circumstances, with the right person, can be the most exhilarating experience in life.'

'But you're the exact opposite of the right person, I can't even see how you can say that with a straight face.'

'*Sí*, I'm the devil. You would never be satisfied with a Normal Norman. You'd be bored rigid in three seconds flat.'

He kissed her before she could countermand his assertion. As first kisses with the devil went, it was soul-stealing and Raven was eternally grateful she was sitting down.

Because Rafael devoured her as if she were his favourite fruit. No millimetre of her mouth went unkissed. When he was done ravaging her lips, he delved between to boldly slide his tongue into her mouth. The toe-curling sensation made her fingers bite hard into his bicep. She needed something solid to hold on to. Unfortunately, Rafael—unyielding, warm— no, hot—heady, sexily irreverent Rafael—was the last anchor she should've been seeking. And yet she couldn't pull away, couldn't summon even the smallest protest as she let him devour her lips.

'*Dios*, you taste even better than I imagined.' He only gave her a chance to snatch a quick breath before he pounced again.

One hand caught her waist, his fingers digging into her flesh to hold her still as he angled his head to go even deeper. Her moan felt ripped from her very soul.

He started to lean her back on the sofa, then he stilled suddenly. Between their lips, the sound of his pained hiss was smothered but Raven recognised it all the same.

Reality came crashing down on her, her dulled brain clamouring to make sense of what she'd let happen. Slowly, painfully, he straightened until he was upright again.

Raven wanted to reach across and help but she was too weak with thwarted lust, too stunned from the realisation that she was still as hopelessly attracted to Rafael as she'd been the first time she was introduced to him as his physiotherapist.

'Shut up,' he ground out hoarsely.

'I didn't say anything.'

'No, but I can hear you thinking. Loudly, noisily. I've never had to compete with a woman mentally working out the Fibonacci Sequence while I was trying to get her naked. And you know what? It's not sexy. It's quite deafeningly unsexy, actually.'

She slid agitated hands into her hair. 'You're being offensive.'

'And you're ruining this electric buzz with all that overthinking. I would much prefer it if you'd shut up and strip for me.'

Her mouth dropped open. Actually dropped opened in a gob-smacked, un-pretty mess that she couldn't stop. 'I really don't know how you managed to snag girlfriend after girlfriend with that insufferable attitude.'

'It's the same way I've snagged you, *piqueña*. It's why you're leaning towards me right now, unable to look away from me as you imagine what it would be like to have me inside you, buried deep, riding us both to ecstasy.'

She jumped back, and her breath whooshed out of her lungs.

'And now you're going to blush.'

As if on cue, heat rose and engulfed her face. 'Crap.'

He laughed, actually laughed at her. Raven had never felt so humiliated. Or so…so hot as he grasped the bottom of his T-shirt.

'Here, I'll go first, shall I? One item of clothing each until we're in flagrante. Deal?'

She wanted to walk out, wanted to tell him what to do with his tight, muscle-packed body and sheer masculine perfection. She wanted to have enough willpower to turn her back on all the things his glinting blue eyes promised. This wasn't her. She wasn't the type of girl who fell casually into sex as if she were choosing the latest hair accessory from a supermarket shelf. So why couldn't she move? Why did every single instinct she had scream at her to move closer to Rafael, to touch, experience the seductive pleasure he promised, instead of running as far as her marathon-trained legs could carry her?

A long-suffering sigh filled with extreme impatience shattered her thoughts. Her gaze sharpened in time to see his hands drop.

'Fine, I get the message. You're about to fall on your puritanical sword, deny yourself pleasure just so you can crawl back into your cold bed and pat yourself on the back. Aren't you?'

'I wasn't…' But she *had* been thinking that, hadn't she? 'Maybe,' she admitted. 'Besides being totally unprofessional, I can't very well advocate no sex for you and then be the one who…who makes you suffer a setback.'

He shook his head, a genuine baffled look on his face. Reaching over carefully, he took her face in his hand. '*Sí*, I get it. More restraint. More suffering for both of us. You're twenty-four so I'm sure you're not a virgin, but are you sure you weren't an inquisitor in a past life?'

Since there was no way she wanted to confirm her virginity, she focused on the second part of his statement. 'I know you don't believe it, but I'm only looking out for you.'

'By torturing me to death? Or is there something else at play here?'

'By making sure you heal as quickly and efficiently as possible.'

He dropped his hand. 'Where's the fun in that?'

Raven kicked herself for immediately missing his touch. 'God, you're unbearable! And what do you mean, "there's something else at play"?'

'Ah. Finally, some fire. Do you have any idea how incredibly hot you look when you're riled?'

Desire dragged low through her abdomen at his heated, husky words. 'You're getting off topic. And that compliment is so clichéd, even a three-year-old wouldn't believe you.'

'Cliché doesn't make it any less true. But yes, I'll get to the point. You like to hide behind a prickly exterior, holding the world at bay because you're afraid.'

'I'm not prickly and I'm most definitely not afraid.'

'You over-think every single move you make.'

'It's called being sensible,' she retorted.

'You're living half a life. Every bone in your body wants to be on the bed with me, yet you're afraid to let yourself just be.'

'Just because I don't put myself about like you doesn't mean I'm not living.'

His lips twisted. 'I wouldn't be this frustrated if I'd been putting it about like you suggest. And don't forget, I was in a coma for several weeks. Have mercy on my poor, withered c—'

'If you finish that sentence I'm walking out of here right now!'

'The C-word offends you?'

'No, your blatant lies do. There's nothing withered or poor about you.'

'*Gracias*…I think.' He tilted his head. 'Now you're about to deflate my ego thoroughly, aren't you?'

'Your ego is Teflon-coated and self-inflating. It doesn't need any help from me.'

He let out an impatient sigh. '*Dios*, Raven, are you going to talk me into another coma or are we going to have a conversation about what's really going on here?'

She shoved her hands onto her hips. 'There's nothing going on. You want to get on with making up for lost time and I happen to be the willing body you've chosen.'

His hands dropped. 'Would it make you feel better if I said yes? It would help you get through the morning-after hand-wringing if you feel righteous anger for being used?'

She gasped. 'I didn't say that.'

He moved further away. 'You didn't have to. *Santa Maria!* We haven't been to bed yet, and already you're seeking excuses to ease your guilt. How long are you going to let your father win?'

Her gasp was a hoarse sound that scraped her throat raw. 'That's low, Rafael.'

'No lower than the way you treat yourself. Have a little pride. You're a beautiful woman, with a powerfully sexual nature you choose to suppress underneath a staid exterior. But, underneath all that togetherness, your true nature is dying to leap out. To be set free.'

'And you're the man to do it? How convenient for you.'

His face remained sober. 'For both of us. I'm willing to rise to the task. I'm very good at it, too. Trust me.'

'Trust you. The self-proclaimed damaged man who is trouble with a capital T?'

'Think of all the experience I'd bring to the task. You couldn't find a better candidate to bed you if you tried.'

She shut her eyes. Despair wove through her because, deep down, she knew he was right. Her body hadn't reacted to anyone this strongly since…heavens, since never! But that was no excuse to throw well-served caution to the wind. 'No. It's not going to happen.'

He was silent for so long her nerves were stretched to the max by the time he spoke. 'What did your father do to you?'

'What makes you think this is about my father, not about an ex?'

'The first cut is the deepest, no?'

She looked around the too posh living room, at the price-less pieces of furniture that most people would give their eye teeth to own.

She didn't belong here. Her presence in Rafael's life was temporary, transient. Baring her soul to a man who didn't possess one was out of the question. Regardless of what she'd told herself she'd seen in his eyes last night, they were nothing more than ships passing in the night.

In a few weeks she would be gone and Rafael would return, healed, to his regular life. 'Yes, the first cut is the deepest, and yes, my father hurt me. Badly. But my scars don't dictate who I am. I am free to choose who to be with, who I have sex with. And I don't want to have it with you.'

CHAPTER SIX

RAFAEL TOOK HER rejection with more grace than she'd given him credit for, especially considering his reaction to her rejection the day of his last X1 race.

Later that day, after shrugging off her terse pronouncement, they strolled into an exclusive rooftop restaurant overlooking Casino Square. Although a whisper of tension flowed between them, Rafael was as charming as ever.

'So, what are your plans after you're done fixing me?' he asked after the first course had been served.

A strange twinge attacked her insides. Pushing it away, she speared her fork through a plump shrimp. 'I'll either get the agency that allocated me the X1 contract to find me another driver to work with, or I'll find one on my own. I could also try the army facility to see if they need a full-time physiotherapist. I have a few possibilities and I figure after you, every other patient would be a breeze to work with.'

Blue eyes gleamed at her across the table. '*Gracias, bonita.*'

She eyed him suspiciously. 'What are you thanking me for, exactly?'

'I've obviously become a yardstick by which you measure your future clients. I consider it an honour.'

She rolled her eyes and found herself grinning when he laughed. Shaking her head, she took another mouthful of her delicious shrimp pasta. 'I knew you were trouble from day one.'

His laughter slowly disappeared. '*Sí,*' he murmured. 'What did you call me? A useless waste of space who was taking up valuable oxygen more worthy human beings were entitled to?'

Her fork clattered onto her plate. 'You remember? Every single word?' she whispered.

His smile was sharp and deadly, the easy camaraderie from moments before completely annihilated as the tension that had lurked solidified into a palpable wall. 'What can I say, *querida*, you cut me to the bone.'

'Was that…was that why…?' She couldn't quite frame the words.

'Why I attempted to turn myself and my car into a Rubik's Cube the next day? Ask me again when I remember anything from the accident.'

She shut her eyes for a brief second, a shudder of guilt and regret raking over her. 'Please believe me, I don't usually lay into anyone quite like that. That day…' She paused, unwilling to bare her whole life to him. But then she realised she owed him an explanation of some sort. 'It was a *very* difficult day.'

'In what way was it difficult?' he probed immediately.

'My mother called me the evening before the race, just before the team dinner where you—'

'When I *dared* to ask you out?' he asked.

Her gaze dropped as she felt a prickle behind her eyelids. 'Her relationship with my father has always been…tempestuous.' That was putting it mildly but she couldn't elaborate any further. 'When she called, she was very upset… She has…moments like that. She wanted to see him. Nothing I said would calm her down. So I called my father—the father I haven't spoken to in years.'

Rafael's brow hitched up a fraction but he didn't interrupt her.

'He wouldn't lift a finger to help. He was too busy, he said. But I could hear the sound of a party in the background. I swallowed my pride and begged him. He refused. When I called my mother to try to explain, her mood…escalated. I was trying to get her some help when you found me and asked me to dinner.'

'So you attempted to slice the skin off my bones because of bad timing?' His words were light but the chilling ice in his eyes told her he hadn't forgiven her. 'What about the dozen times before then?'

She blew out a breath. 'I've just told you the effect my father has on me and on my mother. Do you honestly think I'd ever want to associate myself personally with a man who reminds me of every despicable trait I witnessed growing up?'

'Watch it, *piqueña*,' he murmured softly. 'You didn't think I was despicable when we kissed this morning.'

A wave of heat crept up her face. 'That was a mistake.'

'Also, you may have claws, but I have teeth. Sharp ones and I'm heartless enough to use them.'

She didn't doubt it. For him to have succeeded in securing several championships over the past decade, he had to have a ruthless streak somewhere beneath the indolent playboy demeanour. Certainly, she'd seen his dedication and absolute focus during the racing season.

'I'm sorry, Rafael. But I didn't really understand why you wanted to go out with me. There were dozens more willing girls who would've jumped at the chance to be with you.' If she were being honest, she still didn't understand why he continued to try and goad her into bed. The only thing she could think of was…no, it didn't make sense. 'I'm hardly your Mount Everest.'

'You're not. Been there, done that.'

Her eyes fell to the jagged scar on his forearm. It might have been ugly at one time but now it just blended into the frustratingly captivating masterpiece that was Rafael de Cervantes. 'You've been to a lot of places, done a lot of things.'

'You've been listening to gossip.'

'Before I came to work for you last year, the agency sent me a dossier on you. Is it true that scar on your arm was from a bull goring you?' She pounced on the change of subject all the more because here was her chance to learn more about Rafael.

'*Sí*, and I thanked the bull for the unique, exhilarating experience.'

She suppressed a shudder. 'What is it exactly that you crave? The thrill of the chase? The rush of adrenaline?'

'It's conquering the fear of the unknown.'

His words were so stark, so raw, her breath caught in her lungs.

'What do you mean?'

'I don't like mysteries, *querida*. Take you, for instance. From the moment we met, you held me at arm's length. No woman's ever done that, not effectively anyway, and definitely not for as long as you have, and this isn't arrogance talking. It's just never happened. You were an enigma to me. I wanted to smash aside all your barriers. Instead you built them up higher. You intrigued me to the point I couldn't see anything beyond having you.'

She had never been able to explain the phenomenon of ice and heat that filled her whenever she was in Rafael's presence. She couldn't explain it now the sensation had increased a thousandfold. 'I don't know that I want to be described that way. You make me sound like I'd become your worst nightmare.'

'You had. I wanted to confront it. Turn it into a dream I liked.'

'God, Rafael. Do you hear how twisted that sounds?'

His laugh was nowhere near a normal sound. 'I'm sorry I don't fit your ideal of the right guy.'

'I'm not looking for a right guy. I'm not looking for a guy, period. I just want to do my job.'

'It's not just that though, is it?' He beckoned the waiter and ordered an espresso for himself and a white coffee for her. 'You're here because you want to do penance.'

'And you've been fighting me and trying to drive me away ever since I arrived.'

'If I'd wanted to be rid of you, I would've succeeded.'

'So you want me to stay?'

He shrugged. 'One of the many discoveries I made while stuck in a hospital bed was this—I like being alone. But I don't like being alone in León.'

She sensed the revelation behind the statement. 'Another of your nightmare scenarios?'

He didn't deny it. He just shrugged. 'Tell me more about your mother.'

'Tell me about yours.'

'She's dead.'

In what felt like mere seconds between one and the other, another forceful blow punched through her middle at the stark announcement. 'How—?'

The word stuck in her throat when he shook his head and picked up his newly delivered espresso. 'You're one of a handful of people outside of my family circle I've disclosed that to. It's not a state secret, but it's not a subject I wish to discuss either, so don't ask any more questions. And yes, I know it's hypocritical of me to demand everything from you and give nothing in return, but we both know I do what I like. Your mother?'

She moistened her lips and tried to arrange her thoughts. 'For what it's worth, I'm sorry about your mother.' She sucked in a deep breath and slowly exhaled. All of a sudden, it wasn't so bad to reveal just that little bit more. Because Rafael had shared *something*.

'Mine is alive but barely conscious half the time. You know why? Because she's completely and utterly hung up on a man who can go for months, sometimes years without giving her a single thought. And yet he only has to crook his finger to have her falling into his lap. At least you know your mother loved you. Do you know how devastating it is to find out your own mother would gladly give you away for free if she could have her one true obsession?'

'Is that why you lived with your father?'

'No. Aside from her obsession with my father, she was also diagnosed with severe bipolar disorder when I was seven. For a few years she took the prescribed medication, but as I got older, she would miss a few days here and there. Then days would turn into weeks, then she would stop altogether.'

His frown was thunderous. 'Did you not have any relatives that could step in?'

'None that wanted to add the burden of a pre-teen on top of the responsibilities they already had. And, frankly, I felt I was better off on my own. By ten I could take care of myself. Unfortunately, my mother couldn't. One day she had an episode in a shop. The police were called. Social services got involved. Eventually they tracked down my father and threatened to report him to the authorities when he wouldn't step up.' Bitterness made her throat raw. 'They *made* him take me. And you know what? Every day until I turned eighteen I wished they hadn't.'

'Did he hurt you?' he rasped.

'Not at first. When I initially arrived at his doorstep, he didn't even care enough to resent me for my sudden appearance in his life.' She laughed. 'And he was rich enough that I had my every material need catered for.'

'But?' he demanded.

Ice drenched her skin as the dark memory surged, its oily tentacles reaching for her.

A tinkle of laughter from a table nearby slammed her back into the present. Chilled and exposed, she rubbed her hands over her arms. 'I don't want to relive it, Rafael.'

His jaw tightened. 'It was that bad?'

'Worse.'

His fingers curled around the small, fragile cup in his white knuckled grip before he carefully set it back in its saucer. '*Dios mío*. When did it—?'

'Rafael…please…'

He sucked in a sharp breath, his gaze still fiercely probing as he sat back in his seat. After several seconds, he nodded and pushed back his chair.

Silently he held out his hand. Before the start of the evening she'd have hesitated. But after what she'd shared with him, after seeing his reaction to how she'd grown up, a tiny voice urged her to trust him a little.

She placed her hand in his and let him help her up. 'I should be helping you, not the other way round.'

'Let's forget we're patient and specialist, just for a few hours, *si*?' The low, rough demand made her breath snag in her throat.

When she glanced up at him, he watched her with hooded eyes that held no hint of their usual teasing. Swallowing, she nodded.

They walked in the unseasonably warm evening along the dock that held some of the world's most extravagant and elegant yachts. Or they tried to walk. Rafael was stopped several times along the way by wealthy Monégasques and visiting celebrities. Again and again, Raven tried not to be enthralled by the sight of his breathtaking smile and easy charm. Even when a paparazzo's camera lens flashed nearby he didn't seem to care. But then she caught the clenched fist around his walking stick. She wasn't surprised when he signalled his driver a few moments later.

When she glanced at him, he merely shrugged. 'We have an early flight in the morning. Don't want you to accuse me of depriving you of your beauty sleep.'

She waited until they were in the car, leaving the bright lights of Monte Carlo behind. 'You strive to put a brave face on it all, don't you?'

'A brave face?'

'I saw how the paparazzi affected you just now. And even though you stopped to speak to people, you didn't really want to be there.'

He tilted his head. 'Your powers of deduction are astounding.'

'Don't dismiss me like that, Rafael,' she murmured. 'You've changed.'

Although his expression didn't alter, she saw his shoulders stiffen beneath his expensive cotton shirt.

'Of course I have, *querida*. My hip no longer works and I carry a walking stick.'

'I don't mean physically. You turned away from the cameras at the airport too. You answer their questions but you no longer bask in the limelight. Oh, the playboy is very much a part of your DNA, probably always will be, but…something's changed.'

'*Sí*, I've turned into a decrepit recluse who's been banned from having a bed partner.'

She ignored the quip. 'I bet you're not going to buy that villa, are you?'

The corner of his mouth lifted in a mirthless smile. 'You assume correctly,' he replied, his gaze steady on her face. 'You were right, it's a little too…stalker-ish for me. I think the owner studied what I liked and tried to replicate it without taking the location into consideration. It's slightly creepy, actually. Besides that, Monaco is great for a visit but not somewhere I prefer to live. But then neither is León.'

'Why?'

'Too many bad memories,' he stated.

Somewhere inside, Raven reeled at the easy access he seemed to be giving her. A strong need to know the man made her probe further. 'Your father?'

He paled a little beneath his tan, but he nodded after several seconds. '*Sí*. Amongst other things. He moved to Barcelona after…for a while, but he's back in León now. Seeing him there reminds me of what a disappointment I've been to my family.'

She gasped. 'A disappointment? How…why? You've won eight world championships and ten Constructors' Championships for Team Espíritu. How in the world can that be termed a failure?'

'Those are just trophies, *querida*.'

'Trophies coveted by the some of the world's most disciplined athletes.'

'Why, Raven, I almost think you're trying to make me feel better about myself.'

'You've achieved a lot in your life. Self-deprecation is one thing. Dismissing your achievements out of hand is an insult to the team that has always supported you. Now, if you're talking about your private life…'

'What if I said I was?'

'I've met your father, albeit very briefly. I saw no trace of disappointment when he tried to talk to you. And, as far as I can see, Marco and Sasha worship the ground you walk on, despite you saying you tried to break them up.'

He lifted a hand, his knuckles brushing her cheeks before she knew what he was doing. 'That may have been an over-exaggeration. Was I annoyed when I woke up from my coma to find my best friend had fallen for my brother? *Sí.* But I'm a big boy, I'll learn to adapt. As for worshipping the ground I walk on—appearances can be deceptive. I've done things— things I'm not proud of; things that haunt me in the middle of the night, or in the middle of the day when I smile and shake hands with people who think I'm their golden boy. They don't know what I've done.'

'What have you done, Rafael? Tell me.'

He shook his head, a bleak expression stamped on his face that sent a bolt of apprehension through her.

'Did you notice the condition my father is in?'

She frowned. 'You mean his wheelchair? Of course I did.'

'What if I told you I put him in that wheelchair?'

Rafael looked into her face, trying to read her reaction while at the same time trying to decipher exactly why he was spilling his guts when he never, ever talked about what he'd done eight years ago.

The car passed under a streetlamp and illuminated for a moment her pale, shocked face. 'H…How did you put him in the wheelchair?'

A deep tremor went through him, signalling the rise of the blistering pain that seemed to live just below his skin. 'Take a wild guess.'

'A car accident?'

He nodded, his peculiar fascination with her escalating

when she made a move as if to touch him. At the last moment, she dropped her hand.

'Where did it happen?'

'On the racing track in León. Eight years ago. I walked away unscathed. My father has never walked since.'

This time when she lifted her hand he caught it before she could lower it and twined his around her slender fingers. The surge of pain diminished a little when her fingers tightened.

'I'm so sorry,' she murmured.

His smile felt broken. 'You don't want to know whose fault it was?'

'I'm not going to force you to relive the emotional pain, Rafael. Like you said, I'm not that type of therapist. But one thing I do know is that, contrary to what you might think, your family…your father, from what I saw, is more forgiving than you realise.'

His father might be forgiving of Rafael's role in making him wheelchair-bound, but the other, darker reason would be more unthinkable to forgive. Hell, he hadn't even dreamed of seeking forgiveness. He deserved every baptism of hellfire he lived through every morning when he opened his eyes. 'That's the problem with family. Forgiveness may be readily provided but the crime is never forgotten.'

'Unfortunately, I wouldn't know. Dysfunctional doesn't even apply to me because I had two people who were connected to me by genetics but who were never family.'

The car was drawing up to the villa when he lifted their entwined fingers to his lips. A soft gasp escaped her when he kissed her knuckles. 'Then count yourself lucky.'

Two hours later, Rafael stretched and held in a grimace of pain when he tried to rise from his chair. He eyed the walking stick leaning against his desk and with an impatient hand he reached for it.

Pelvis, fractured in three places…broken leg…multiple cracked ribs…severe brain swelling…lucky to be alive.

The doctor's recital of his injuries when he'd woken from his coma should've shocked him. It hadn't. He'd known for as long as he could remember that he had the luck of the devil. He'd exploited that trait mercilessly when he was younger, and then honed it into becoming the best racing driver around when he was older. No matter how many hairy situations he put himself in, he seemed to come out, if not completely whole, then alive.

Recalling his conversation earlier with Raven, he paused in the hallway. *I'm not going to force you to relive the emotional pain.*

Little did she know that he relived it every waking moment and most nights in his vivid nightmares. He might have cheated death countless times, but his penance was to relive the devastation he'd brought to his family over and over again.

His phone pinged and before he glanced at it he knew who it was.

His father...

He deleted the message, unread. *Dios*, even if they wanted to grant it, who was he to accept their forgiveness—?

The sound in the library next to his study attracted his attention.

Raven's lusciously heady perfume drew him to the room before he could stop himself. 'It's almost midnight. What are you doing up?'

'I was looking for something to read. The only reading material I have upstairs is boring clinical stuff, and my tablet is charging, so...'

He glanced down at the papers in his hand. He had no idea what he was doing, no idea where this project would take him but... He debated for a few seconds and made up his mind. Closing the distance between them, he stopped in front of her.

'Here.' He tossed a bound sheaf of papers at her, which she managed to catch before they spilled everywhere.

'What is this?'

One corner of his mouth lifted in a dangerous little half-smile that always made her forget to breathe. 'Two articles for *X1 Magazine*…and something new I'm working on.'

'Something new? I didn't know you wrote outside of your monthly *CEO's Snippets*.'

He shrugged. 'Three months ago—while I was trussed up like a turkey in a hospital bed—I was approached by a couple of publishing houses to write my memoirs.' He laughed. 'I guess they figured a has-been like me would jump at the chance to lay it all out there before the moths set in.'

She glanced down at the thick inch of paper between her fingers. 'And you agreed?' she asked as she started to leaf through the pages.

'I said I'd think about it. I had time on my hands after all.'

She read, then read some more. On the third page, she looked up. 'This isn't your memoirs, unless you were a girl who grew up in Valencia in the late forties.'

'*Bonita*, you're getting ahead of yourself. *Por favor*, contain yourself and let me finish.'

She stared up at him. Rafael gave himself a mental slap against the need to keep staring into those mesmerising eyes. 'I started writing and realised fiction suited me much better than non-fiction. I told them no to the memoir.'

'And?' she prompted when he lapsed into silence. 'You told them about this?'

'No. I've told no one about this. Except you.'

Surprise registered in her eyes before she glanced back down at the papers. 'Are you sure you want me to read it?'

'It's pure fiction. No deep, dark secrets in there for you to hold over my head.'

Wide hazel eyes, alluring and daring at the same time, rose to lock on his. 'Are you sure?'

'If you're thinking of flipping through the pages for X-rated material, I'm afraid you'll be disappointed.'

Her blush was a slow wave of heat that he wanted to trace with his fingers. For a woman so fierce in her dedication to her craft and so determined to succeed despite her past, she blushed with an innocence that made him painfully erect. Despite his intense discomfort, he wanted to continue to bait her so she blushed for him again.

Unable to help himself, he lowered his gaze to the shallow rise and fall of her chest.

When she cleared her throat delicately, he forced his gaze upwards. 'So what are you looking for—an honest critique? I'm sure I can read whatever it is you've written and give an honest view, if that's what you want?'

He smiled at her prim tone and forced himself to step back before he gave in to the need to kiss her. Their kiss had only opened up a craving to experience the heady sensation again. But, aside from the insane physical attraction, he was feeling a peculiar pull to Raven Blass he wasn't completely comfortable with.

Keeping his distance from her was impossible considering her role in his life, but he wasn't a hormonal teenager any longer and he refused to make any move towards her that reminded her of her sleazebag father.

If anything was going to happen between them, Raven had to make the first move…or indicate in clear and precise terms that she wanted him to.

'*Gracias*, it is. I await your thoughts on my efforts with bated breath.'

CHAPTER SEVEN

THEIR EARLY MORNING departure to Italy, accompanied by Rafael's executive assistant and a trio of ex-racers, meant that Raven had no chance to discuss Rafael's manuscript with him at any point. A fact for which she was more than thankful.

The story of the young girl was both uplifting and heartbreaking. Rafael's language was lyrical and poignant, clever and funny in a way that had made her feel each and every word, every expression.

Reading his work, she'd felt just that little bit closer to him. Raven wasn't sure if she was more frightened or insane for feeling like that. It was that floundering feeling that had made her take a seat as far away from Rafael as possible.

But even though she made the right noises with the guy next to her—whose name she couldn't immediately remember—she couldn't get Rafael's story out of her head.

Nor could she deny his talent. She'd learned very early on, after reading an unauthorised biography on him before accepting the job as his physiotherapist last year, that Rafael had a magic touch in most endeavours he undertook in his life. That he'd dedicated his life to racing had only meant that the sport had benefited endlessly.

His regular contribution to X1 Premier Management's monthly magazine already garnered a subscription said to be in the millions. If he chose to dedicate his life to writing fiction his fan base would become insane.

And you would probably be his adoring number one fan.

Without warning, Rafael's gaze swung towards her. The sizzling *knowledge* in that look sent sharp arrows of need racing to her pelvis. Her pulse hammered at her throat, her skin tingling with the chemistry of what she felt for Rafael.

'...you ever been to Monza?' The German ex-racer seated next to her—Axel Jung, she remembered his name now—stared at her with blatant interest.

She shook her head but couldn't tear her gaze away from the formidable, intensely charismatic man whose gaze held her prisoner from across the aisle. 'Um, no, I was Rafael's physio last year but Monza wasn't on the race calendar so I missed it.'

'You're in for a treat. It's one of the best racetracks in the world.'

She swallowed and tried to dismiss the intensity of Rafael's stare. 'Yes, so I've been told. The old track was even more spectacular, from the pictures I've seen of it.'

Axel's chuckle helped her break eye contact with Rafael but not before she saw his gaze swing to Axel and back to her.

'If you liked danger with your spectacular view, that was the track to race on,' Axel said.

She made an effort to turn her attention to him and almost regretted it when she glimpsed his deepening interest. 'I suspect that's why it's a thrill for most drivers?' she ventured.

He nodded eagerly. 'I don't know a driver who hasn't dreamt of driving at Monza, either on the old or the new track. The tickets for Monza's All-Star event sold out within minutes of going online.'

Raven had a feeling it had something to do with Rafael's presence, this being one of his first public appearances since his accident. 'That's great for the charity, then?'

'Yes, it is. I'd be honoured if you'll permit me to show you around Monza.' He drew closer. His smile widened, lending his blond-haired, blue-eyed features a boyish charm.

'I'm there to work, I'm afraid. And you'll be driving I expect?'

Axel, a two-time world champion twenty-five years ago, nodded. 'Rafael and I have a friendly rivalry that seems to draw the crowd.' He laughed. The fondness in his voice was clear. 'He's a special one, that one. The playboy thing is just a front. Don't let it fool you. Deep down, there beats the heart of a genius forged in steel. A fierce leader who would fight to the death for what he believes in.'

Having her instincts confirmed that there was more to Rafael than met the eye made her slow to respond. A quick glance at him showed him in deep conversation with a member of his All-Star team. 'I...'

'He single-handedly brought the board members to his way of thinking two years ago when they tried to put off new safety measures for drivers,' Axel said.

'*Safety?*' Raven asked in surprise. 'But I thought...'

'You think because we love speed and hurtle around race-tracks at two hundred and fifty miles per hour we think less of safety? Ask any driver. The opposite is true. We manage to take the risks we do *because* of people like Rafael and the work they do to ensure drivers' safety.'

Feeling wave after wave of astonishment roll through her, she glanced again at Rafael, only to find his attention fixed on her, his blue eyes narrowed to speculative slits. He glanced away again and resumed his conversation.

The floundering feeling escalated. 'Excuse me,' she murmured to Axel when the stewardess entered to take drinks orders. Standing, she made her way towards the large bedroom and the en suite bathroom.

After splashing water on her wrists, she re-knotted her hair in a secure bun and left the bathroom, only to stumble to a halt.

Rafael stood, back braced solidly against the bedroom door. His presence in the enclosed space, larger than life and equally as imposing, dried her mouth.

Heart hammering, she stayed where she was, away from the danger radiating from him. 'I...is there something you need?'

He folded his arms and angled his head. '*Need?* No.' He remained in front of the door.

Raven licked her lips and immediately regretted it. 'Can we return to the cabin, then?'

'Not just yet,' he rasped, then just stood there, watching her with a predatory gleam that made her nape tighten.

Silence stretched for several minutes as he stayed put, seemingly in no hurry to go anywhere, or speak, for that matter.

She searched her mind for what he could possibly want, and felt her heart lurch with disappointment. 'You're not in here because you want to make sure your playboy status is intact, are you?'

'What was Axel saying to you?'

She waved him away. 'Nothing for you to worry about.' He remained in place, that infuriatingly well-defined eyebrow arched. 'Okay, if you must know, he told me that beneath all that lady-killer persona, you're really a Boy Scout. Oh, and he also offered to show me Monza.'

He glanced away but she saw his jaw tighten. 'I hope you told him no?'

'Maybe.' She started to move towards him in the hope that he'd get the hint and move. He remained, rock-still and immovable.

'Stay away from him,' he said, his voice low but no less forcefully lethal.

Her pulse spiked higher. 'Sexually, socially or just for the hell of it?'

With a swiftness she wouldn't have attributed to him considering his injuries, he reached forward, grabbed her arms, whirled her round and reversed their position. Her lungs expended their oxygen supply as she found herself trapped between the hard, polished wood and Rafael's equally hard, warm body.

One hand gripped her nape while the other settled firmly on her waist. Heat ratcheted several notches. Inhaling only made matters worse because Rafael's scent, potent and delicious, attacked her senses with rabid fervour.

'He was looking at you as if he wanted to serve you up on his sauerkraut.'

'And what, you're jealous?'

'Not if you tell me you're not thinking of falling into the clutches of an ex-racer more than twice your age.'

'Axel's only in his mid-forties. And I'm touched you're looking out for me.'

Blue eyes deepened by his blue long-sleeved shirt and navy jeans narrowed even further. 'And he also likes to think he's slick with the ladies.'

'Scared of the competition?'

'Scared I'm going to have to toss his ass out of the plane without a parachute if you don't tell me you'll stay away from him.' Without warning, one thigh wedged between hers. The heat emanating from him made her whole body feel as if it were on fire. Second by inexorable second, he pressed closer against her. His hard chest brushed against hers, stinging sensitive nipples to life. Raven fought a moan and tried to decide whether defiance or acquiescence was her best path.

'Is this what it means to be caught between a rock and a hard place?' she asked, unable to resist baiting him just a little.

His laugh sent a skitter of pleasure through her. 'You're making jokes, *querida*?'

'You're laughing, aren't you?'

'*Sí*,' he agreed. The hand on her waist moved a fraction higher, dug deeper in an almost possessive hold on her ribcage. 'But I'm still waiting for an answer.'

A small voice cautioned her against throwing more fuel onto the flames.

'I spoke to him for fifteen minutes, but I barely remember what he looks like,' she whispered against seriously tempting lips a hair's breadth from hers. 'But why do you care? Really?'

'You were the first person I told about my father outside my family. You haven't condemned me…yet. In my own small way, I'm trying to return the favour by saving you from a potentially unfortunate situation.'

'By trapping me here and threatening to toss a man out of the plane?'

'It's my Latin blood, *piqueña*. It takes me from zero to

growly in less than five seconds.' He closed the gap between their lips and their bodies.

A fervid moan rose from her chest as sensation crashed over her head. Her knees turned liquid and she would've lost her balance had she not been trapped so powerfully against a towering pile of formidable maleness. As they were, with his thigh wedged so firmly between hers, she felt the heat from his leg caress her intimately. Friction, urgent and undeniable, made her pulse race faster. Even more when his tongue delved between her lips. Like the first time they'd kissed, Rafael seemed bent on devouring her. Although she'd been kissed, she'd never been kissed quite like this, with a dedication so intense she felt as if she were being consumed.

When he finally let her up for air, it was to allow her a single breath before he pounced again. Her hands, which had miraculously risen to glide over his shoulders, finally found the wherewithal to push him away.

'Rafael…'

'No, not yet.' His lips swooped, but she managed to turn her head just in time. He settled for nibbling the corner of her mouth, a caress so erotic she throbbed low down with the sensation.

'We need to stop. Everyone out there will think we're in here…doing…having…'

'Sex…saying it doesn't make you a dirty, dirty girl, Raven.' His thigh moved, inserting itself even more firmly between hers. Again friction caused sensation to explode in her belly.

She flushed. 'I know that.'

'Then say it,' he commanded, pulling back to stare into her eyes.

Defiance surged back on a wave of desperation. 'Sex. Sex, sex, *sex*—'

He kissed her silent, and damn, but did she enjoy it. When he finally raised his head she was thoroughly and dangerously breathless. 'It's okay, you've made your point. Although I can't say that'll dissuade our fellow travellers from thinking we've joined the Mile High Club.'

A growl of frustration rumbled out before she could stop it. 'Why couldn't you leave this alone until we landed?'

'The same reason you're still caressing my shoulders even though you're protesting my presence here with you.'

She dropped her hands and swore she could feel her skin tingling in protest.

'I...this is crazy,' she muttered under her breath.

'Sí, but we can't help ourselves where the other is concerned. Are you ready to go back?'

A shaky nod was all she could manage before he withdrew his thigh from between hers. The loss of his support and heat made her want to cry out in protest. She stopped herself in time and checked to see if her buttons had come undone.

With a sigh of relief, she stepped away from the door.

Rafael was very close behind her when they exited the bedroom. 'You didn't tell me what you thought of the story.'

She looked over her shoulder. 'I thought it was incredible.'

He stilled, an arrested look on his face. 'You enjoyed it?'

'Very much. The girl has an amazing spirit. I can't wait to find out more about her journey.' She glanced at him. 'That is if you intend to continue with it?'

A look passed over his face, gone too quickly before she could decipher it. 'With such a rousing endorsement, how could I not? As it happens, I have a few more chapters.'

Pleasure fizzed through her. 'Will you let me read it?'

He smiled. 'You mean you want to read more, despite the lack of X-rated material?'

She huffed in irritation. 'Why did I think a lovely conversation with you would last more than five seconds?'

His low laugh curled around her senses. She was so lost in it, she didn't realise he had led her away from Axel until he pushed her into the seat next to his.

The Monza circuit, perched on the outskirts of the small namesake town, was situated north of Milan. The view from above as Rafael's helicopter pilot flew over the racetrack was spectacular.

A riot of colour from the different sponsor logos and team colours defied the late winter greyness. She felt the palpable excitement from small teams readying the race cars before they landed.

Casting a glance at Rafael, she couldn't immediately see his reaction due to wraparound shades and noise-cancelling headphones, but his shoulders, the same ones she'd caressed barely ninety minutes ago, tensed the closer they got to the landing pad. If they'd been alone she would've placed her hand on his—an incredible development considering this time last week the thought of touching him set her teeth on edge—but she didn't want to attract undue attention. The paddock would supply enough gossip to fuel this event and the rest of the X1 season as it was.

Cameras flashed as soon as the helicopter touched down and demanding questions were lobbed towards them the moment the doors opened.

Are you returning to racing, Rafael?

Will you be officially announcing your retirement today or is this the start of your comeback?

Is it true you're suffering from post-traumatic stress disorder?

His jaw was set in concrete even though his lips were curved in a smile as he stepped out of the helicopter and waved a lazy hand at the cameras.

A luxurious four-by-four was parked a few feet away. He held the door open for Raven and slid in after her.

'I don't know how you can stand them without wanting to punch someone in the face,' Raven found herself murmuring as she watched a particularly ambitious paparazzo hop onto the back of a scooter and race after them.

'They help raise the profile of the sport. They're a necessary evil.'

'Even when they're intrusive to the point of personal violation?'

'When I engage them, I engage them on my terms. It's a skill I learned early.'

With a surprise, she realised that everything the press knew about Rafael was something he'd chosen to share with them, not some sleazy gossip they'd dug up. To the common spectator, Rafael lived his life in the public eye but in the past few weeks she'd discovered he had secrets…secrets he shared with no one, not even his family.

'You give them just enough to keep them interested and to keep them from prying deeper.'

Stunning blue eyes returned her stare with amusement and a hint of respect. 'That is just so, my clever Raven.'

'So, what pierces that armour, Rafael?'

His smile dimmed. 'I could tell you but I'd have to sleep with you.'

Raven's heart lurched and then sped up when, for a single second, she found herself contemplating if that was a barter worth considering. *Sleeping with Rafael…*

A tiny electric shock that zapped her system left her speechless.

'Since you're not slapping my face in outrage, dare I hope the suggestion isn't as repulsive as you found it previously?'

'I…I never thought you were repulsive,' she replied. 'You may have been a little too intense with your interest, that's all.'

'You dislike my intensity?'

She opened her mouth to say *yes,* and found herself pausing. 'I wasn't used to it. And I didn't like that you had everyone falling over themselves for you and yet you weren't satisfied.'

'But now we've spent some time together you think you *understand* me?' His tone held a hint of derision that chilled her a little.

'I don't claim to understand you but I think I know you a little better, yes.'

The warmth slowly left his eyes to be replaced by a look so neutral he seemed like a total stranger.

Their vehicle pulled up in front of the expansive, stunning motor home that had been set up to accommodate the Italian All-Star event. Several dignitaries from the sports world waited to greet Rafael. He reached for the door handle and turned to her before alighting.

'Don't let that knowledge go to your head, *querida*. I'd hate for you to be disappointed once you realise I won't hesitate to take advantage of that little chink in your armour. Underneath all this, there is only a core of nothingness that will stun you to your soul.'

He got out before she could respond. Before she drew another breath, he'd transformed into Rafael de Cervantes, world champion and charm aficionado. She watched women and *men* fall over themselves to be in his company. Basking in the adoration, he disappeared into the motor home without a backward glance.

Rafael waved away yet another offer of vintage champagne and cast his gaze around for Raven.

He'd been too harsh, he knew. Had he—finally—scared her away for good? The thought didn't please him as it should have.

But she'd strayed far too close, encroaching on a deep dark place he liked to keep to himself. He hadn't been joking when he'd warned her about the core of nothingness. How could he? What would be the point in revealing that grotesque, unthinkable secret?

She would hate you, and you don't want that.

His gut tightened but he pushed the thought away.

No one could hate him more than he hated himself. It was better that he ensured Raven harboured no illusions. Although she'd probably claim not to be, she was the type to see the good in everyone. If she didn't she wouldn't have asked for help from a deplorable father who had subjected her to *dios* knew what to save her mother. He suspected that, deep down, she'd hoped her father would reveal himself to be something other than he was.

Rafael wasn't and would never be a knight in shining armour. Not to her and not to any other woman. He took what he wanted and he didn't give a damn.

Above the heads of the two men he was talking to, he saw Chantilly enter the room on her husband's arm. She zeroed in on him with an openly predatory look, her heavily made-up eyes promising filthy decadence.

Rafael felt nothing. Or rather he felt…different. On further examining his reaction, he realised the sensation he was feeling wasn't the cheap thrill of playing games with Sergey's wife. It was self-loathing for having played it in the first place.

He looked away without acknowledging her look and cast his gaze around the room one more time. Realising he still searched for Raven—where the hell was she?—he made a sound of impatience under his breath.

'Is everything all right?' the chairman of the All-Star event asked him.

'The old racetrack has been carefully inspected as I requested?'

The white-haired man nodded. 'Of course. Every single inch of it. You still haven't told us whether you'll be participating.'

Tightness seized his chest. He forced himself to take a breath and smile. 'The event is only beginning, Adriano. I'll let you old folks have some fun first.'

'Less of the old, if you please.'

The laughter smoothed over his non-answer but the tightness didn't decrease. Nor did his temper when he looked up a third time and found Raven standing at the far end of the room with Axel.

She'd changed from jeans into yet another pair of trousers, made of a faintly shimmery material, and a black clingy top that threw her gym-fit body into relief when she moved.

The sound of a nearby engine revving provided the perfect excuse for Axel to lean in closer to whisper into her ear.
Whatever the German was saying to her had her smiling and
nodding. Obviously encouraged, her companion moved even
closer, one hand brushing her shoulder as he spoke.

Rafael moved without recognising an intention to do so,
a feat in itself considering his hip was growing stiffer from
standing for too long. 'Raven, there you are.'

She turned to him. 'Did you want me?' she asked, then
flushed slightly.

'Of course I want you,' he replied. 'Why else are you here,
if not to come when I want you?'

A spurt of anger entered her eyes. 'What can I do for you?'

'I need your physio services. What else?'

She frowned. 'According to your itinerary, you're working
until ten o'clock tonight. Which is why I scheduled a swim
therapy for you afterwards and a proper physio session in the
morning.'

His eyes stayed on hers. 'My schedule is fluid and right
now I need you.'

'Ah, actually, I'm glad you're here, Rafael,' Axel said.

'Really? And why's that, Jung?'

The other man cleared his throat. 'I was hoping to convince
you to let my team borrow Raven's services for a few hours.
Our regular physiotherapist came down with a stomach bug
and had to stay at the hotel.'

'Out of the question,' Rafael replied without a single glance
in his direction.

'Rafael!'

'Need I remind you what your contract states?' he asked
her.

'I don't need reminding, but surely—'

He shifted sideways deliberately in a move to get her attention. And succeeded immediately. 'What happened?' she
demanded, her keen eyes trailing down his body, making a
visual inspection.

'You were right. This whole thing has simply worn me out. I think I'll have an early night.' He turned towards the door. 'Are you coming?'

'I…yes, of course.' Concern was etched into her face. Rafael wanted to reassure her that his hip wasn't painful enough to warrant that level of worry.

But he didn't because he couldn't guarantee that she wouldn't wish to stay, return to Axel. The disconcerting feeling unsettled him further.

'I was away for just over an hour. Please tell me you didn't try and do anything foolish to your body in that time.'

'Where were you, exactly?'

'Excuse me?'

'Were you with Jung all that time?' he asked, an unfamiliar feeling in his chest.

'Are we seriously doing this again?'

'How else would he have got it into his mind to poach you?'

'He wasn't…isn't trying to poach me. He was telling the truth. His team's physio was sent back to his hotel because he fell ill. But they think it's just a twenty-four hour virus. I didn't see the harm in agreeing to give my professional opinion.'

'You should've spoken to me first.'

'In the mood you were in? You bit my head off because I got too close again. I won't be your personal punchbag for whenever you feel the need to strike out.'

He sucked in a weary breath and Raven forced herself to look at him properly for the first time. Not that it was a hardship.

It was clear he was in pain. His skin was slightly clammy and stress lines flared from his eyes. 'What the hell did you do to yourself?' she asked softly.

'You should've stuck around if you were concerned.'

She didn't get the opportunity to answer as they'd arrived at the helipad. The blades were already whirring when she took her seat beside Rafael for the short trip to their hotel in Milan.

As they exited the lift towards their exclusive penthouse suite, she turned to him. 'Lean on me.'

When he didn't argue or make a suggestive comment, she knew he was suffering. Raven was thankful she'd had the forethought to ring ahead to make sure the equipment she needed had been set up.

Back in their hotel, after Rafael stripped to his boxers, she started with a firm sports massage to relax his limbs before she went to work on the strained hip muscles.

By the time she was done, a fine sheen of sweat had broken over his face. Pouring a glass of water, she handed it to him.

He drank and handed the glass back to her.

'I don't like seeing you with other men. It drives me slightly nuts,' he said abruptly.

She stilled in the act of putting away a weighted leg brace. 'You can't have all the toys in the playground, Rafael.'

'I just want one toy. The one sitting on top of the tree that everyone says I can't have.'

'What you can't do is to keep shaking the tree in the hope that the toy will fall into your lap. That's cheating.'

'It's not cheating; it's taking the initiative. Anyway, you can't be with Axel.'

She stopped, head tilted to the side, before she tucked a strand of hair behind one ear. 'Okay, I'll play. Why can't I be with him?'

He gave a pained grimace. 'He has a ridiculous name, for a start. Think how ridiculous your future kids would find you. Raven and Axel Jung. Doesn't rhyme.'

'And I have to have a man whose name rhymes with mine, why?'

'Synergy in all things. Take you and me.'

'You and me?' she parroted.

'*Sí*. Rafa and Raven rolls right off the tongue. It was meant to be.'

She passed him a towel. 'I'd suspect you were on some sort

of high, but you didn't touch a drop of alcohol at the mixer and you've refused any pain medication.'

'I'm completely rational. And completely right.'

'It must be hunger making you delirious then.' She handed him the walking stick and walked beside him to the living room. 'Room service?'

With a sigh, he sank into the nearest wide velvet sofa, nodded and put his head back on the chair.

'What would you like?' she asked.

'You choose.'

'Would you like me to spoon-feed you when it arrives, too?'

His grin was a study in mind-melting hotness and unashamed sexual arrogance. 'You're not the first to offer, *querida*. But I may just make you the first to succeed in that task.'

Rolling her eyes, she ordered two steaks with a green salad for them. Then, on impulse, she ordered a Côte du Rhone.

The wine wouldn't exactly lay him flat but it might let him relax enough to get a good night's sleep, especially since he refused to take any medication.

After she'd placed the order, she set the phone down and approached the seating area.

Rafael patted the space beside him.

Very deliberately, and sensibly, she thought, she chose the seat furthest from him and ignored his low mocking laugh.

'So, care to tell me what happened today?'

He stilled, then his eyes grew hooded. 'First day back on the job. Everyone was clamouring for the boss.'

Raven got the feeling it was a little bit more than that but she wisely kept it to herself. 'What are the races in aid of this year?' she asked, changing the subject.

He tensed further, wrong-footing her assumption that this was a safe subject.

For the longest time, she thought he wouldn't answer. 'XPM started a foundation five years ago for the victims of road accidents and their families. But we soon realised that giving away money doesn't really help. Educating about safety was a better route to go. So we've extended the programme to testing road and vehicle safety, with special concentration on young drivers.'

'Was…was it because of what happened with your father?'

His eyes darkened. 'Surprisingly, no. It was because a boy racer wiped out a family of six because he wasn't aware of how powerful the machine underneath him really was. I knew exactly how powerful the car I drove was so my transgression didn't come from ignorance.'

'Where did it come from?'

'Arrogance. Pride. I owned the world and could do as I pleased, including ignoring signs of danger.' His face remained impassive, this slightly self-loathing playboy who wore his faults freely on his chest and dared the world to judge him. His phone rang just then. He checked the screen, tensed and pressed the off button. 'Speak of the devil and he appears,' he murmured. His voice was low and pensive with an unmistakable thread of pain.

Raven frowned. 'That was your father?'

'*Sí*,' he replied simply.

'And you didn't answer.'

The eyes he raised to her were dark and stormy. 'I didn't want to interrupt our stimulating conversation. You were saying…?'

She searched her memory banks and tried to pull together the threads of what they'd been talking about. 'You used the past tense when you said you owned the world? You no longer think that?'

'World domination is overrated. Mo' power mo' problems.' Although he smiled, the tortured pain remained.

'Is that why you won't forgive yourself? Because you think you should've known better.'

'My, my, is it Psychology 101?'

She pressed her lips together. 'It is, isn't it?'

'If I said yes, would you make it all better?'

'If you said yes you would feel better all on your own.' The doorbell rang and she looked towards the door. 'Think about that while I serve our feast.'

The emotions raging within him didn't disappear from his eyes as she went to the door to let the waiter in.

By unspoken agreement they stuck to safer subjects as they ate—once again, Rafael taking her refusal to feed him with equanimity.

When she refused a second glass of wine, he set the bottle down and twirled his glass, his gaze focused on the contents.

'So where is this island of yours that Marco and Sasha have gone to?'

'There are a string of islands near Great Exuma. We own one of them.'

'Wow, what does it feel like to own your own island?'

'Much like it feels to own a car, or a handbag, or a pen. They're all just possessions.'

'Possessions most people spend their lives dreaming about.'

'Are you one of those people? Do you dream of finding a man to take you from your everyday drudgery to a life filled with luxury?'

'First of all, I don't consider what I do drudgery. Secondly, while I think dreams are worth having, I set more store by the hard work that *propels* the achievement of that dream.'

'So I can't sway you with the promise of a private island of your very own?'

'Nah, I have a thing about private islands.'

His brow rose. 'A *thing*?'

She nodded. 'I saw a TV show once where a group of people crashed onto one and spent a hellishly long time trying to get off the damned rock.' Her mock shudder made him grin. 'A concrete jungle and the promise of a mocha latte every morning suits me just fine.'

He raised his glass. 'To concrete jungles and the euphoria of wall-to-wall coffee shops.'

'Indeed.' She clinked glasses with him. Then it dawned

on her how easy the atmosphere had become between them; how much more she wanted to stay where she was, getting to know this compelling man who spelled trouble for her. The thought forced her to push her chair back. 'I think I'll head to bed now. Goodnight, Rafael.'

If he noticed the sudden chill in her voice, he didn't react to it. 'Before you go, I have something for you,' he said, pointing to the elegant console table that stood outside the suite's study.

Seeing the neat stack of papers, Raven felt a leap of pleasure. Going to the table, she picked up the papers and, sure enough, it was the continuation of Ana's story.

'Did you write all of this last night?' she asked him.

He shrugged. 'The muse struck when I was awake. No big deal.' But she could tell it was. His gaze was hooded and his smile a little tight. It was almost…almost as if he was nervous about her reading it.

'Thanks for trusting me with this, Rafael.'

He looked startled for a moment, then he nodded. '*De nada. Buenas noches, bonita,*' he replied simply.

The distinct lack of *naughty* left her floundering for a moment. Then she forced herself to walk towards her suite.

'Raven?' His voice stopped her beside the wide, elegant double doors leading into the hallway. When she turned, his gaze had dropped to assess the contents of his wine glass.

'Yes?'

'Don't flirt with Jung.'

Her pulse raced. Later, when she was safely in her cool bed, she tried to convince herself it was the effects of the wine that made her say, 'Quid pro quo, my friend. If I'm not allowed to flirt, then no more numbers on your walking stick. Agreed?'

Blue eyes lifted, regarded her steadily, their brilliance and intensity as unnerving as they'd been the very first time she'd looked into them. After a full minute, he nodded. 'Agreed.'

CHAPTER EIGHT

SHE FOUND HIM in the penthouse pool the next morning. She stood, awestruck, as Rafael cleaved the water in rapid, powerful strokes, his sleek muscles moving in perfect symmetry. He turned his head just before he dived under and executed a turn and, for a split second, Raven became the focus of piercing blue eyes.

One length, two lengths…three.

After completing the fourth, he stopped at the far end, flipped onto this back and swam lazily towards her. 'Are you going to stand there all day or are you going to join in? We leave for the racetrack in half an hour.'

'I'm not coming in, thank you. We were supposed to have a full physio session this morning.'

'I was up and raring to go, *bonita*. You were not.'

It was the first time ever that Raven had overslept or been late for an appointment. She couldn't stem the heat that crawled up into her face as she recalled the reason why. When she'd found herself unable to sleep, she'd opened up Rafael's manuscript and delved back between the pages. If anything, the story had been even better the second time round, renewed fascination with Ana, the heroine, keeping her awake.

'I was only ten minutes late.'

He stopped on the step just beneath where she stood and sluiced a hand through his hair. 'Ten throwaway minutes to you is a lifetime to me.' He hauled himself out of the pool. Raven couldn't stop herself from ogling extremely well-toned biceps and a tight, streamlined body. Even the scars he'd sustained on his legs and especially his hip were filled with character that made her want to trace her fingers over it, test his skin's texture for herself.

She forced herself to look away before the fierce flames rising could totally engulf her. He grabbed the towel she tossed to him and rubbed it lazily over his body.

'Well, since you had the full therapy session last night, I don't see the harm in reversing the regime.'

He glanced over and winked. 'My thoughts exactly.'

Suspicion skittered along her spine. 'You're surprisingly chipper this morning.' Looking closer, she saw that his face had lost its strained edge, and when he turned to toss the towel aside, his movement had lost last night's stiffness.

'It's amazing what a good night's sleep can do. I feel as if I have a new lease of life.' He picked up his walking stick and came towards her, a sexy, melt-your-panties-off grin firmly in place. 'Come, we'll have breakfast and I can tell you how to make your tardiness up to me.'

'Anything less than a pound of flesh and I'll probably die of shock,' she muttered.

He laughed. The sound floated along her skin then sank in with pleasure-giving intensity. 'You wound me. I was thinking more along the lines of your thoughts on the manuscript.'

She didn't answer immediately. She was too caught up in watching the ripple of muscle as he sauntered out of the pool area—and through his bedroom, where discarded clothes and twisted sheets made her temperature rise higher—towards the sun-dappled balcony where their breakfast had been laid out.

Goodness knew how she managed not to stare like some hormonal schoolgirl.

'Wow, should I take your silence to mean it was sheer dross?'

Focus! She sat down at the table, snapped out her napkin and laid it over her lap, wishing she could throw a blanket over her erotic thoughts just as easily.

He poured her coffee—mocha latte—and added a dash of cinnamon, just the way she liked it. Raven decided she was *not* going to read anything into Rafael's intimate knowledge of how she took her caffeine. But inside she felt a long held-in tightness spring free, accompanied by the faintest spark of fear.

'It wasn't dross. I'm sure you know that. I love Ana's transition from girl into woman. And that first meeting with Carlos was what every girl dreams of. I'm happy she's putting her dark past behind her...'

'But?' He scythed through her ambivalence.

'But I think Carlos is coming on too strong, too fast. He risks overwhelming Ana just a little bit.'

He picked up his own coffee and eyed her over the rim. 'But I think she has a backbone of steel. Do you not think she has what it takes to stay?'

Raven nodded. 'I think she does. She sees him as a challenge...welcomes it to some extent, but I'm still a little scared for her.'

'You're invested in her. Which is what a writer wants, isn't it? Maybe she needs to be pushed out of her comfort zone to see what she really wants.'

'I notice she likes racing, just like Carlos.'

He stilled. '*Sí*. It is a racing thriller, after all.'

Raven carefully set her cup down and picked up a slice of toast. 'She wouldn't, by chance, be modelled on your sister-in-law, would she?' she asked, keeping her voice level.

He shrugged. 'Sasha is one of the best female drivers I've known. What's your point?'

She didn't know how to articulate what it made her feel. Hell, she couldn't grasp the roiling feelings herself. All she knew was that she didn't want Rafael to be thinking of a specific woman when he wrote the story.

'I just think you would appeal to a wider audience if the character wasn't so...specific.'

'You mean, it would appeal to you?'

The toast fell from her hand. 'I don't know what you mean.'

'Are you going to play this game? Really?'

The words, so similar to those she'd thrown at him, made heat crawl up her face. 'Fine. Touché.' She hardened her spine and forced out the next words. 'But you know what I'm try-ing to say.'

'Are we still talking about my manuscript?' he asked, a trace of a smile on his lips.

'We've taken a slight detour.'

'A detour that touches on our…friendship and the adjust-ments I need to make in order for it to advance?'

Her hands shook at how quickly they'd strayed into dan-gerous territory. She couldn't look into his probing gaze so she studiously buttered her toast. 'Y…yes.'

He stayed silent for so long she was forced to glance up. Blue eyes pinned her to her chair. 'Don't expect me to turn into something I'm not, *querida*.'

'Take a first step. You might surprise yourself.'

'And you, *pequeña*, how are you surprising yourself?'

The question, unexpected and lightning-quick, sent a bolt of shock through her. She floundered, unsure of what to say. 'I…I'm not sure…'

'Well, make sure. If I'm to bend over backwards to accom-modate you, you have to give something back, *sí*?'

That pulse of fear intensified. Opening up to Rafael in Mo-naco, telling him things she'd never told another human soul, had left her feeling raw and exposed.

Now, by daring her in his oh-so-sexy way to open up even more, he threatened to take it a whole lot further, luring her with a promise she knew deep down he wouldn't keep. That was the essence of playboys. They exuded charisma, invited confidences until they had you in their grasp.

And yet the rare glimpses she'd caught of Rafael threatened that long-held belief. He was alluding to the fact that playboys could have hearts of gold. Raven wasn't sure she was ready to handle that nugget of information.

For years, her mother had believed it—believed it still—and look where it'd got her. If she let Rafael in and he did a number on her, she wasn't sure who she would hate more—Rafael…or herself.

'You don't have to turn into something else. All I ask is to see a little bit more, make my choice with a clear, if not total, view of the facts. Because I can't have sex with you for the sake of it. I would hate myself and I would hate you.'

'Ah, but we're already having sex, *mi amor*. All that's left is for our bodies to catch up.'

Of course, she could *really* have done without that thought in her head. Because, suddenly, it was all she could think about.

She walked beside Rafael along the long paddock an hour later, watching as he stopped at every single All-Star garage to greet and exchange info with the crew. From her stint as his physio last year, Raven knew just how meticulous a driver he was. He understood the minutiae of racing to the last detail and could probably recite the inner workings of a turbo engine in his sleep.

Which was why his accident, judged to be the result of human error—his—had stunned everyone. Some had speculated that it had been the effects of partying hard that had finally done him in. But, in the last few weeks, she'd caught occasional glimpses of the man underneath and knew Rafael de Cervantes wasn't all gloss. He rarely drank more than a glass of champagne at any event and she knew he'd banned smoking in the paddock a few years back.

What she didn't know was how deep the Rafael de Cervantes well ran, or how monstrous the demons were that chased him. It was clear he was haunted by something in his past. At first she'd thought it was his father. But even though that particular revelation had been painful to him, it had been when she'd mentioned his mother that the real pain had surfaced, just for a moment.

She glanced at him, a little overwhelmed by the many facets she had previously been too riled up to see. Rafael had traits she abhorred, traits that reminded her of the man whose DNA ran through her veins.

But he was also so much more.

'I can hear you thinking again.'

'Unfortunately, my active brain cells refuse to subside into bimbo mode just because I'm in your presence.' She cast a telling glance at a groupie who'd just obtained an autograph and was squealing in delight as she ran to her friends.

'You can wow me with your superior intelligence later,' he said as they approached the last garage in the paddock.

The first thing she noticed was the age group of this particular crew. Aside from two older supervisors, everyone else ranged from early to late teens. The other thing that struck her was their synchronicity and clear pride in what they were doing.

When Rafael greeted them, they responded as if he were their supreme deity come to life. She wasn't surprised by their reaction. What surprised her was Rafael's almost bashful response as they gathered around him. Then it all disappeared as he started to speak. Started to teach.

They hung on his every word, and took turns asking him challenging questions, which he threw right back to them. Respect shone from their eyes and the depth of understanding he'd managed to impart in the space of the hour before the race started left Raven reeling.

'Close your mouth, *piqueña*. You'll catch flies,' he quipped as he led her away from the garage towards the VIP Paddock Club.

Her mouth snapped shut. 'That was incredible, the way you got them to listen, got them to apply knowledge they'd forgotten they had.'

'They're a talented bunch. And they love racing. All there is to learn is a respect for speed.' He shrugged. 'It wasn't hard.'

'No. You're a natural teacher.'

'I learned from the best.'

'Marco?'

He shook his head and held the door open to let her into the lift that whisked them up to the top floor VIP lounge. From there they had a panoramic view over the entire race circuit.

Rafael bypassed several A-listers who'd paid thousands of euros to attend this exclusive event and led her into a private roped-off area. He held out a chair for her then sat down opposite her. 'My father. He gave me my first go-kart when I was five. There's nothing about engines that he doesn't know. By the time I was nine, I could dismantle and reassemble a carburetor without assistance.'

'I didn't know your father raced.'

'He didn't. My grandfather had a small hotel business and wanted my father to study business so he could help him run it. But he never lost his love of racing. The moment his business grew successful enough, he enrolled Marco, then me in learning the sport. And he took us to all the European races, much to my mother's distress.'

The pang of envy for what she'd never had made her feel small so she pushed it away. Especially given what she knew of the strain between father and son now.

'That sounds just like what happened to Carlos in your story.'

He glanced at her with a tense smile. 'Does it?'

'Yes.' When he just shrugged, she decided not to pursue the subject of his story. 'So your father took you to all the races? Sounds like an idyllic childhood.'

'Sure, if you're prepared to forgive the fact that back then I was so intent on winning I didn't feel any compunction in crashing into every single car in front of me just to put them out of business. I was disqualified more times than I actually won races.'

'But I'm guessing your father persevered. He saw the raw talent and did everything he could to nurture it.' Something her own father hadn't even come close to attempting with her.

'*Sí*, he showed me the difference between winning at all costs and winning with integrity. And I repaid that by making sure he would never be able to drive a car again.' His face was taut with pain, his eyes bleak with a haunting expression that cracked across her heart.

'I saw how things were between you two at Jack's christening, but have you spoken to him at all since the accident?'

He tensed, waited for the waiter who'd brought their drinks to leave before he answered. 'Of course I have.'

'I mean about what happened.'

'What would be the point?'

'To find out how he feels about it?'

'How he *feels*? Trust me, I have a fair idea.'

Recalling the look on his father's face, she shook her head. 'Maybe you don't. Perhaps you should talk to him again. Or maybe let *him* talk to you. He could have something to say to you instead of you thinking it only works the other way round.'

He frowned suddenly. 'You're head shrinking me again. And how the hell did we get onto this subject anyway? It's boring me.'

'Don't,' she said softly.

A glaze of ice sharpened his blue eyes. 'Don't what?'

'Don't trivialise it. You'll have to tackle it sooner or later.'

'Like you have tackled your father?'

Her breath shut off in her chest. 'This is different.'

'How?' He had to raise his voice to be heard over the sound of engines leaving the garages to line up on the racetrack. Rafael barely glanced at them, his attention riveted on her face.

'Despite everything that's happened, your father loves you enough to want to connect with you. My father doesn't care if I'm alive or dead. He never has, and he never will.'

Rafael saw the depth of pain that slashed across her features before she turned to watch the action unfolding on the racetrack. He wanted to say something, but found he had no words of wisdom or of comfort to give her.

Because he didn't agree with the redeeming quality she seemed to want to find in him. He had no doubt that if she knew the extent of his sins, she wouldn't be so quick to offer her comfort.

An icy vice threatened to crush his chest, just as it did every time he thought of his mother. He'd awoken this morning with her screams ringing in his ears, the image of her lifeless eyes imprinted on his retinas.

No, he had no words of comfort. He'd trashed everything good in his life, and had come close to dismantling his relationship with his brother last year. The last thing he wanted to do was admit to Raven that part of his refusal to speak to his father was because he didn't want to discover whether he was irredeemably trashed in his father's eyes too.

His gaze flicked to the cars lining up on the track. Unlike the normal grand prix races when the cars lined up according to their qualifying time, the six All-Star cars were lined up side by side.

Team El Camino's red and black racer, driven by the young driver he'd been working with, was the first off the mark. Rafael felt a spurt of pride, which he immediately doused.

He had no right to feel pride. All he'd done was take what his father had taught him and passed it on. His father deserved the credit here, not him.

'Don't be so hard on yourself.'

Irrational anger sprang up within him. The fact that she seemed so determined to make him feel better when she was content to wallow in her own *daddy issues* filled him with anger. The fact that he was sexually frustrated—heck, he was going on eight months without having had sex—was setting his teeth on edge. The fact that he was up here, cooling his heels when he wanted more than anything to be down there... behind the wheel of a racing car—

Ice chilled his veins as he acknowledged the full extent of what he was feeling.

'Rafael?'

He didn't respond or turn towards her. Instead he watched the screen as Axel Jung threatened to take the lead from the young driver.

'Rafael, are you okay?'

'Do me a favour, *querida*, and stop talking. You're holding a mirror up to my numerous flaws. There's only so much
I can take before I have to revert to type. And since you don't
want that, I suggest you let me absorb a few of them and concentrate on enjoying this race, *si*?'

Far from doing what he expected of her, which was to
retreat into sullen silence or—from experience with other
women—flounce off in feminine affront, she merely picked
up the remote that operated the giant screen in their section
and turned it on. Then she picked up the menu, asked him
what he wanted for lunch, then ordered it for them, her face
set in smooth, neutral lines.

He waited several minutes, despising the emotion that ate
away his insides like acid on metal. Guilt. An emotion he
didn't like to acknowledge.

Guilt for upsetting her. 'I'm sorry,' he said.

A shapely eyebrow lifted in his direction, then she nodded.
'It's okay. I don't like dredging up my past either. I guess I
should learn to respect yours.'

'But I seem to invite you to dig, which is very unlike me.'
He frowned.

A tiny, perfect smile played around lips he remembered
tasting. A craving such as he'd never known punched through
him. Right in that moment, all he wanted to do was taste her
again. Keep on tasting her until there were no clothes between
them. Then he would taste her in the most elemental way possible. Right between her legs.

He would so enjoy watching her come. Again and again.
And again.

Normally, he would have been thrilled by the natural path
of his thoughts, but Rafael admitted his need held a previously
unknown edge to it…an almost desperate craving he'd never
experienced before. He wanted Raven. And yet a part of him
was terrified by the depth of his need.

Forcing himself not to analyse it too closely, he returned

his attention to the track and felt a further spurt of discontentment when he saw Axel Jung had taken the lead.

Lunch was delivered and they ate in truce-like silence.

When Axel Jung took the race by a half second, Rafael tried to force back his black mood. As the CEO of the company organising the event, he had to step up to the podium and say a few words.

'If your jaw tightens any further, you'll do yourself an injury,' Raven murmured next to him.

'I'm smiling, *querida*, like the great racer slash CEO that I am,' he muttered back, turning towards her.

This close, her perfume filled his nostrils and invaded his senses. She gave a laugh and raised a sceptical brow. 'We both know you want to throw your toys out of the pram because the team you silently support came second. You're supposed to be unbiased, remember?'

He moved closer to her, felt the brush of her arm against his side and the depth of need intensified. 'I am unbiased. I just wanted my young driver to win, that's all,' he said, unrepentant.

Her teasing laugh and the way she bumped his shoulder in playful admonition unravelled him further. He glanced down into her face and his breath strangled at her breathtaking beauty.

A shout made him turn. Axel had stepped off the podium and was making his way towards them. Or Raven in particular, if the interest in his eyes was anything to go by.

Before conscious thought formed, Rafael moved, deliberately blocking the German from accessing the woman beside him. *His woman.*

'Congratulations, Jung. I think the press want their interview now.' He deftly turned the German towards the waiting paparazzi. As moves went, Rafael thought it was supremely smooth, but Raven's gasp told him the grace had been lost on her.

'Did you just do what I think you did?'

'That depends. Did you want him to come over here and slobber all over you?'

She shuddered. 'No, but I'm not sure I wanted a blatant territory-marking from you either.'

He wanted to tell her that he wished the whole paddock knew to keep away from her. But he knew it wouldn't go down well. It would also point out just how much he detested the idea of Raven with any other man. 'Point taken.'

Her eyes widened. 'Wow, I'm not sure whether to feel suspicious or special that you've conceded a point to me.'

'You should feel special.' His gaze trapped and held hers. 'Very special.'

Raven returned his stare, trying to summon a tiny bit of ire beneath all the high octane, breath-stealing emotions coursing through her. But the excitement licking along her nerve endings put the effort to shame.

Something of her feelings must have shown on her face because his eyes darkened dramatically. His gaze dropped to her lips, the heated pulse beating a wild rhythm in her neck, then back to her face.

Calmly, he breathed out and gave her a slow, electrifying smile. Eyes still locked on hers, he pulled out his phone and spoke in clear tones. Unfortunately, Spanish wasn't her forte so she had no clue what he was saying. But she made out the word *avión,* which made her even more curious.

'What was that about?' she asked when he hung up.

'I've arranged for our things to be packed. I thought we might head to Mexico a couple of days earlier than the rest of the racers.'

'Won't you be needed?'

'Possibly, but for the next two days I'm taking your advice and delegating. Does this make you happy?'

There was a deeper question beneath the stated one, a hungry gleam in his eyes that boldly proclaimed his intention should she agree to what he was proposing.

In a single heartbeat, Raven accepted it. 'Yes.'

It was almost a relief to let go of the angst and the rigid control. At least for a while. She knew without a shadow of a doubt that it would return a hundredfold soon enough.

CHAPTER NINE

SHE WAS GOING to take a lover. She was going to lose her virginity to the very man she'd run a mile from last year. The man who would most likely break her heart into a tiny million pieces long before this thing between them was over.

Nerves threatened to eat her up as their tiny seaplane banked and headed towards the private beachfront of the stunning villa Rafael owned in Los Cabos, Mexico. By now she knew all about the eighteen-bedroom villa, the lower level sauna and steam room, the two swimming pools and the names of every member of the construction crew who'd built the villa to Rafael's exact specification three years ago.

Because she'd needed to babble, to fill her head with white noise to distract her from the urge to spill the fact that she hadn't done this before. The closer they drew to their destination, the higher panic had flared beneath the surface of her outward calm.

Rafael's experience with women was world-renowned. What if she made a spectacular fool of herself? What if he was so put off by her inexperience he recoiled from her? To silence the voices, she babbled some more, found out that he had a staff of five who managed the villa and that he practised his handicap on the legendary golf course nearby when the occasion suited him.

In direct contrast to her nervous chirping, Rafael had been circumspect, his watchful silence unlike anything she'd ever known. Although he'd answered her questions with inexhaustible patience, his eyes had remained riveted on her the whole time, occasionally dropping to her lips as if he couldn't wait to taste, to devour.

They touched down on the water and powered to a stop next

to a large wooden jetty. After alighting, they headed towards an open-topped jeep for the short drive to the villa.

Even though she felt as if she knew the property inside and out, Raven wasn't prepared for the sheer, jaw-dropping beauty of the adobe white-washed walls, the highly polished exposed beams and almost ever-present sea views from the windows of the mission-style villa. Spanish-influenced paintings adorned the walls, lending a rich tapestry to the luxurious interior.

In her bedroom, rich fabrics in earthy colours formed the backdrop to a mostly white theme set against warm terracotta floors. But one item drew her attention.

'What's this for?' She touched the black high-powered telescope that stood before one large window.

He came and stood behind her, bringing that warm, evocative scent that she'd come to associate with him and only him. It took an insane amount of willpower not to lean back into his hard-packed body.

'The waters around here are well-known grounds for sperm whales. They tend to come closer to shore first thing in the morning. If you're lucky you'll spot a few while we're here.'

Again the sombre, almost guarded response caught her off-guard. She glanced at him over her shoulder. He returned her stare with an intensity that made her breath catch. After a full minute, he lifted his hand and drifted warm fingers down her cheek in a soothing, belly-melting gesture.

'You're nervous, *bonita*. Don't be. I promise it will be good.'

Her laugh was aimed at herself as much as at him. 'That's easy for you to say.'

His finger touched and stayed on the pulse jumping in her throat. 'It isn't. I haven't done this for a long time, too. Hell, I don't know if the equipment works.'

He gave a wry smile when her brows shot up. 'You don't?'

'You will be the first since a while before the accident.'

'But I felt...I know you...'

'Can get a hard-on? *Sí*, but I'm yet to test the practical integrity of the machinery.'

'Oh, so I'm to be your guinea pig?' she teased, a little appeased that she wasn't the only one climbing walls about the prospect of them together.

'Guinea pigs don't have mouths like yours, or eyes the colour of a desert oasis. Or breasts that cry out to be suckled. Or the most perfect heart-shaped ass that makes me want to put you face down and straddle—'

'Okay, I get it. I'm hotter than a Greek furnace.' Her eyes strayed to the perfectly made up bed, her imagination running wild. She swallowed. 'I...I'd like a tour of the outside now, if you don't mind.'

His finger drifted up to the corner of her mouth, pressed gently before he put his finger to his own lips and groaned.

'If that's what you want.'

She nodded.

He didn't heed her request right away. He leaned down, placed his lips at the juncture between her neck and shoulder and ran his tongue over her thundering pulse. He answered her groan with one of his own, then he reluctantly stepped back. Raven was glad when he offered his arm because her legs had grown decidedly shaky.

The heeled leather boots she'd worn with her jeans and black-edged white shirt clicked alongside his heavier tread as they went outside.

On one side, an extensive stretch of grass led to a large thatched poolside bar surrounded by potted palm trees.

Beside it, an area clearly designated for relaxing featured a hot tub under long bales of white linen that had been intertwined to form a stunning canopy that offered shade. After the chill of Europe, it was a balm to feel the sun on her face.

'Come, there's something I want to show you.' There was heated anticipation in the low rumble that fluttered over her skin, feeding her own sizzling emotions.

Rafael led her across the grass and down shallow steps to

the private, secluded beach. All through the tour, his hand had been drifting up and down her back, stealing her thoughts and playing havoc with her pulse.

Which meant that she was totally unprepared for the sight that confronted her when he led her round a rock-sheltered cove.

The thick timber four-poster canopy had been erected right on the shore, with a massive day bed suspended by thick intertwined ropes. The sight was so vividly breathtaking, and so unexpectedly raw and pagan, she stopped in her tracks.

There was only one reason for the bed.

Sex. Outdoor sex.

Heat engulfed her whole body as Rafael's gaze met and trapped hers.

'The high rocks shield even the most determined lenses. And see those?' He indicated three discreetly placed floodlights pointing out towards the water. 'They come on at night and send a glare out to sea so any cunning paparazzi out there get nothing but glare when they try and get pictures of the villa.'

She swallowed hard. 'Even so, I can't imagine doing…it so blatantly.'

He caught her hand in his and kissed her palm. 'Never say never. Now, I believe we have a therapy session to work through?'

The fact that she'd forgotten her main reason for being there made her uncomfortable.

She hastened to cover it up. 'Yes, and don't hate me, but we'll need to step things up a bit.'

'Do with me what you will, *querida*. I'm but putty in your hands.'

He led the way back into the villa and into his bedroom. The setting sun threw orange shades across the king-size wooden-framed bed that seemed to dominate the room. When he threw his walking stick on the exquisitely designed recliner facing the double doors leading to a large balcony, she was reminded again why she was here with Rafael in the first place.

She'd cautioned him against sex only a handful of days ago, and yet here she was, unable to think beyond the raging need to strip every piece of clothing from his body.

Guilt ate away inside her.

'I can hear you thinking again. And I don't feel warm and fuzzy about the direction of your thoughts.' He started to unbutton his shirt.

She tried and failed not to let her eyes linger over his muscular chest and down over his washboard stomach, following the faint line of hair that disappeared beneath his jeans.

'Is this where we hold hands and pray about whether we should have sex or not?'

He was back. The irreverent, sexy, endlessly charismatic man who had women the world over falling at his feet.

Or was he?

A careful look into his eyes showed not the gleam of irreverence but a quietly speculative look beneath his words. 'Are you afraid you'll hate sex with me? Or afraid you'll love it so much you'll beg to become a groupie?'

She shook her head. 'As much as I want it to be easy, I've never taken a decision lightly. And I don't think you should either. It's not just me I'm thinking about here, Rafael. What if all this turns around on you? What if we do this and you get even more damaged?'

'Then I'll learn to live with it. Come here,' he said, holding out his hand. Although his mouth was smiling, his eyes held a very firm command.

She had to dig her toes in to stay put. 'You'll live with it because you think you deserve all the bad things that happen to you?'

His smile slowly eroded until only a trace remained. 'Raven, it's time to stop being my therapist and just be my lover.'

'Rafael…'

'Come. Here.'

He held still, hands outstretched. Almost against her will, she found herself moving forward. He waited until she was within touching distance. Then he lunged for her, sliding his fingers between hers to entrap her.

With his other hand he pulled her close, his fingers spreading over her bottom. Moving forward, he backed her against the wall, enclosing her thighs between his. 'I've got you now. No escape. Now, are you going to undress or do you need help?'

She gnawed on her lower lip, rioting emotions tearing her apart. 'I was so sure I wanted this, Rafael, but I'll never forgive myself if I make things worse for you—'

He growled, 'Damn it, just get naked, will you?'

When she remained still, he took the task into his own hands. For a man who hadn't slept with a woman for almost a year, he didn't seem to lack the skill needed to undress her.

She was down to her bra and knickers within seconds. One deft flick of his fingers disposed of her bra. Slowly he took one step back, then another.

'*Dios*, I knew you would be worth it,' he rasped, his fiercely intent gaze making her skin heat up and pucker in all the right places. Grabbing her by the waist, he reversed their positions and walked her back towards the bed. At the back of her mind she knew she needed to tell him about her lack of experience. But words were in short supply when confronted with the perfection that was Rafael's muscled torso.

With one firm push, she lay sprawled on the bed. He placed one knee on the bed, pushed forward, then winced as he positioned himself over her.

Her concerned gasp drowned beneath his kiss. The kiss that rocked her to her very soul. His tongue pushed inside, warm, insistent and pulse-melting as he showed her the extent of his mastery. Unable to bear the torrent of sensation, she jerked, her hands flailing as she tried to find purchase. He moved over her, pinned her more firmly to the bed with his hips flush against her. When he winced again, she wrenched her mouth from his.

'Before you say it, I'm fine. Dampen the mood with another virtuous monologue and I will spank you. Hard.'

She flushed deep and fierce, but it didn't keep her silent. 'I can't…I can't stop caring about your well-being just because it's inconvenient for you. Just tell me if you're okay.'

'I'm okay. But if I had to, I'd cut off my arm just to be inside you, to feel you close around me like you'd never let me go.'

'Bloody hell, do you practice those lines or do they really just fall off your lips?'

'If I plan to relaunch myself as a multimillion euro best-selling writer, *bonita*, then a way with words is a must.' He sobered. 'But that doesn't mean I don't mean them. I mean every single word I say to you.'

Her heart stuttered, then thundered wildly. 'Rafael…' Her eyes drifted shut.

'I'm lethal. I know.' He settled himself more firmly until she felt his rigid size against the fabric of her knickers. He rocked forward and the relentless pressure on her clitoris made a few dozen stars explode behind her closed eyelids.

'You're beyond lethal,' she breathed shakily. 'You're everything I should be running away from.'

His mouth drifted down her cheek to her jaw and back again. He pressed another kiss to the corner of her mouth, then she felt him move away. 'Hey, open your eyes.'

Reluctantly, she obeyed, already missing his mouth on her.

His gaze was solemn. 'Don't run, Raven. I'm broken and cannot chase after you. Not just yet.'

Her breath caught. 'Would you really? Chase after me?'

'Most definitely. Because I get extremely grumpy when I'm cheated out of an orgasm.'

The slap she aimed at his arm was half-hearted because his mouth was descending to wreak havoc on hers once more. When he finally allowed her to breathe, she was mindless with pleasure.

'I've wanted you for so long, I can't remember when I didn't want you.'

'But…why? Because I was the only paddock bunny who wouldn't fall into your bed?'

She expected a clever quip about his irresistibility. Instead, his gaze turned serious. 'Because within that tainted, false existence, you managed to remain pure. Nothing touched you. I craved that purity. I wanted to touch it, to see what it felt like. But you wouldn't even give me the time of day.'

'Because you had enough groupies hanging around you. I…I also thought you were with Sasha.'

He groaned. 'I guess I played the playboy game a little too well.'

'You mean you weren't?'

'I grew jaded a long time ago but some cloaks are more difficult to cast off than others.'

At her half-snort, he laughed. 'Do you know this is the longest I've been in a bedroom with a woman without one of us halfway to an orgasm?'

She knew that he meant the woman, not him. 'How trying for you.'

He pushed against her once more, his erection a fierce, rigid presence. '*Sí.* It's very trying. You should do something about it before my poor body gives out.' He trailed his mouth over hers before planting a row of kisses along her jaw.

'You really are incorrigible,' she gasped.

'Yes, I am,' he murmured, slowly licking his way down her neck to her pulse. 'I am incorrigible. And I deserve to be punished. Mercilessly.' He slid a hand to caress her belly, then lower to boldly cup her. 'Show me who's boss, my stern, sensible Raven. Give me the punishment I deserve.'

Her breath snagged in her chest. The same chest where her heart hammered like a piston about to burst its casing.

His fingers pressed harder, rhythmic, unrelenting. This time the explosion of heat stemmed from her very core and radiated throughout her body. Her legs parted wider, inviting him to embed himself even deeper. Her restless fingers traced the line of his jeans and found firm skin. Her fingers slipped an inch beneath and he moaned. The sound vibrated along her nerves as heat oozed between her legs.

Her hips undulated in sync with the movement of his fingers, and in that moment, Raven felt as if she were melting from the inside out. She moaned at the intensity of it.

'That's it, *precioso*, give it up for me,' he murmured in her ear, then bit on her lobe. Her cry echoed in the room, the sound as alien to her as the feelings coursing through her body. When his hot mouth trailed down her neck, over her shoulder blades, she held her breath, at once dreading and anticipating the sensation of his stubble roughness on her breast.

With a hungry lunge, he sucked one nipple into his mouth and drew hard on it. At the same time, one firm finger pressed on her most sensitive spot.

'Oh God!' Pleasure exploded in a fiery sensation that made her hips buck straight off the bed. She felt Rafael move off her and alongside her, but the pressure of his fingers and mouth didn't abate. Her climax dragged out until she feared she would expire from it. When her tremors subsided, he left her breasts to plant a forceful kiss on her lips. She fought to breathe.

Heavens, he was too much.

She opened her eyes to find his gaze on hers, intense and purposeful. 'If you're thinking of concocting a means of escape now you've come, know now I have no intention of letting that happen.'

'Why would I want to escape? Unless I'm mistaken, the best is yet to come. Yes?'

The relieved exhalation made her guess he'd suspected she was feeling overwhelmed. 'You have no idea. Kiss me.'

Raven's fingers curled into his nape, glorying in the luxurious heat of his skin as she complied with the heated request.

No, she didn't want to escape. Touching him felt so good, so incredibly pleasurable, that fleeing was the last thing on her mind. The thought surprised her, almost tripping out of her mouth. She curbed it in time. Rafael's head was already swollen by the thought that he could turn her on. Admitting how totally enthralled she was by him would make him even more insufferable. Although, the way she was feeling right now, she wouldn't be surprised if his sharp intellect worked it out before long—

'You're thinking again.'

She stared into blue eyes filled with raw hunger and masculine affront. Slowly she let her fingers drift through his hair, experiencing a keen sense of feminine satisfaction when he groaned. 'What are you going to do about it?'

His lips parted in a feral smile. 'Don't challenge a man on the knife-edge of need, sweetheart. You might regret it. If you survive the consequences.'

Without giving her time to answer, he pulled her down on top of him, both hands imprisoning her to his body as he fell back on the bed. Unerringly, his mouth found hers.

Raven stopped thinking.

And gave herself over to sensation. Rafael's pelvic bone might have been broken and pieced back together but there was nothing wrong with his arms. He lifted her above him and held her in place while he feasted on her breasts. When he was done, he lifted even higher. 'Take off your panties for me.'

With shaky fingers she drew them off, experienced a momentary stab of self-consciousness, which was promptly washed away when he positioned her legs on either side of him and looked up at her.

'You might want to hold onto something,' he murmured huskily, taking a sharp bite of the tender skin of her inner thigh.

The statement wasn't a casual boast. At the first brush of his tongue on her sex, her whole body arched and shook. She would've catapulted off him had he not been holding her hips in an iron grip.

Pain shot through fingers which had grasped the wooden

headboard at his warning. He licked, sucked and tortured her with a skill that left her reeling and hanging on for dear life.

When she tumbled headlong into another firestorm, he caught her in his arms and caressed her body until she could breathe again. Then he left her for a moment.

The sound of foil ripping drew her hazy gaze to him. The sight of his erection in his fist made her sex swell all over again.

He caught her stare and sent her a lethal smile. 'Next time, you get to do it.'

Raven didn't know what to do with that. Nor did she know how to find the correct words to tell him she'd never done it before. In the end, they just spilled out.

'Rafael, I'm a virgin.'

He stilled, shock darkening his eyes. A look flitted through his eyes a second before he shut them. The hand he raked through his hair was decidedly shaky.

He sucked in a long harsh breath, then opened his eyes. The raw hunger hadn't abated but the fisted, white-knuckled hand on his thigh showed he was making an inhuman effort to contain it. 'Do you want to stop?' he rasped, jaw clenched as he fought for control.

The thought of stopping made her insides scream in rejection. 'No. I don't. But I wanted you to know before…before it happened.'

He exhaled slowly. His hand unclenched, then clenched again as his gaze slid hungrily over her. 'I can guess your reasons for remaining celibate. What happened to you would make anyone swear off sex. I know the chemistry between us is insane, but you need to be sure you want to do this now, with me.'

'Would you rather I do it with someone else?' she quipped lightly, although the very thought of anyone but Rafael touching her made her shudder in rejection.

He lunged for her, firm hands grasping her shoulders in a rigid hold before she could take another breath.

'Not unless that *someone else* wishes to get his throat ripped out,' he bit out. He pinned her to the bed and devoured her with an anger-tinged, lethally aroused intensity that made fire roar through her body.

By the time he parted her legs and looked deep into her eyes, she was almost lost.

'I'd planned for you to be on top our first time. But I think this will be easier on you.'

His bent arms caged her as he probed her entrance, his gaze searching hers with every inch he slid inside her. The momentary tightening that made her breath catch stilled his forward momentum.

'Raven?' he croaked, tension screaming through his body as he framed her face in gentle hands.

'I'm okay.'

'That makes one of us.'

Her fingers tried to smooth back his hair but the silky strands refused to stay in place. 'I…can I do anything?'

His laugh was tinged with pain. '*Sí*, you could stop being so damned sexy.' He pushed another fraction and her breath hitched again. '*Dios*, I'm sorry,' he murmured, bending to place a reverent kiss on her lips.

Raven didn't know what was in store for her but she knew her body was screaming with the need to find out. With a deep breath—because, hell, no pain no gain—she pushed her hip upward. His cursed groan met her hiss of pain, which quickly disappeared to be replaced by a feeling so phenomenal words failed her.

'Raven!' Rafael's response was half praise, half reproach.

Tentatively, she moved again.

He growled. 'Damn it, woman. *Stay still.*'

'Why?'

'Because this will be over sooner than you'd like if you don't.'

Heart hammering, she inhaled and gasped when the tips

of her breasts brushed his sweat-filmed chest. 'But at least we know the equipment is working, right?'

He pushed the last few inches until he was firmly seated inside her. Sensation as she'd never known flooded her. At her cry of delight, he pulled out slowly and repeated the thrust. Her head slammed back against the pillow, her fingers clenching hard in his hair as she held on for mercy.

Yep, there was nothing faulty in Rafael's equipment.

With another hungry groan, he increased the tempo, murmuring hot, erotic encouragement in her ear as she started to meet his hips with tiny thrusts of her own.

This time when she came the explosion was so forceful, so completely annihilating, she wasn't sure whether she would ever recover.

Rafael plucked her hands from his hair and pinned them on the bed, then proceeded to dominate her senses once more until she was orgasming again and again.

When she heard his final guttural groan of release, she was sure she'd gone insane with pleasure overload.

'*Dios*...' His voice was rough. Mildly shocked. 'This must be what heaven feels like.'

A bolt of pleasure, pure and true, went through her.

Don't get carried away, Raven.

To bring herself down to earth, she searched her mind for something innocuous to say.

'If you break out into *At Last*, I'll personally make sure you never walk again.'

His laugh was deep, full and extremely contagious. She found herself joining in as he collapsed onto his side and pulled her body into his.

They laughed until they were both out of breath. Then he fisted a hand through her hair and tugged her face up to his. After kissing her breathless, he released her.

'I was thinking more along the lines of *Again and Again and Again*. If there's a song like that, I'll need to learn the lyrics. If there isn't I might need to write one.' He cupped her nape and pulled her down for another unending kiss that left her breathless and seriously afraid for her sanity. 'I love kissing you,' he rasped.

A bolt of something strong and unfamiliar went through her, followed swiftly by a threat of apprehension. Steadying a hand on his chest, she pulled herself up.

'Where do you think you're going?' he asked.

She averted her gaze from his and fought to find reason in all this madness. 'I need to get up.'

'No. You need to look after me, and my needs demand that, after what you've just done to me, I stay in this bed. Which means you have to stay too.'

Unable to resist, she glanced down his body and swallowed the hungry need that coursed through her. It was unthinkable that she would want him again, so voraciously, so soon. But she did.

'If you carry on licking your lips and eyeing me like that, I'll have to teach you this lesson all over again.'

She blinked. 'I can't…we can't…it's too soon.'

'As you rightly noted, the equipment works so I most certainly can, *pequeña*.' He moved and she saw his fleeting grimace. 'But maybe you need to go on top this time.' He held out his hand and she swayed towards him.

'This is crazy, Rafael,' she protested feebly, even as she let him arrange her over him.

'But crazy good, no?'

She melted into his arms. 'Crazy good, yes.'

'Tell me what really happened with your father. What did he do to make you yearn for your eighteenth birthday?'

Rafael couldn't believe the words tumbling out of his mouth. But then again, he couldn't believe a lot that had happened in the last twenty-four hours. From the moment he'd placed the phone call to set things in motion to fly them to Mexico, he'd felt control and reason slipping out of his grasp.

Not that he'd had much in the way of control when it came

to the woman drifting in and out of sleep only a heartbeat away. Sure, he used the Los Cabos villa for entertaining. But it was mostly on business, never for pleasure. And he'd never let a woman stay over. Until now.

Her raven-black hair spread over his arm and he couldn't resist putting his nose to the silky strands, inhaling the peach-scented shampoo as he waited for the answer to the question that invited shared confidences he wasn't sure he wanted to reciprocate. But what the hell? She'd pried more information out of him in the last few weeks than he'd ever released in years.

A little reciprocity didn't hurt.

She turned towards him and spoke in a low, quiet voice. 'Remember I told you he barely acknowledged my existence at first?'

He nodded.

'Over time, as I got older, that began to change. I noticed from the way he looked at me. I thought I was imagining it. Then I overheard the housekeeper saying something to my father's driver.'

'What did she say?'

'That my father didn't really believe I was his daughter. I couldn't be because I looked nothing like him—he has ash-blond hair and blue eyes. I inherited my mother's colouring. Between fourteen and fifteen, I shot up in height and grew breasts. I tried not to link that and the fact that he'd started entertaining more and more at his house instead of at his private club.'

Rafael's hand tightened into a fist out of her sight and he fought to maintain a regular breathing pattern as she continued.

'He encouraged me to stay up at the weekend, help him *host* his parties. When I refused, he got angry, but he didn't take his anger out on me. The housekeeper's son, who was the general handyman, got fired when my father saw me talking to him, then the gardener went, then his driver of fifteen years. I got the hint and decided to do as I was told. By the time I turned sixteen, he was entertaining a few nights during the week and most weekends, and the outfits he wanted me to wear to those parties got…skimpier.'

Rafael's sucked-in breath made her glance up, her eyes wary. Swiftly he kissed her and nudged her nose with his to continue. But the white-hot rage inside him blazed higher.

'I knew I had to do something. I asked for the housekeeper's help, even though I knew I was putting her livelihood in jeopardy. Luckily, she was willing to help. We forged my father's signature and got a DNA test done. When the results came I showed them to him. He was angry, of course, but he couldn't refute the evidence any longer.'

'And did things get better?'

She shrugged but Rafael knew the gesture was anything but uncaring. 'For a time, he reverted to his old, cold indifference. I was hoping he'd take his partying out of the house but they continued…'

Her lids descended and he saw her lips tremble. Spearing his fingers in her hair, he tilted her face until she was forced to look at him. Haunting memory lurked in the green depths. 'Raven, what happened?'

'His…his male friends began to take notice of me.'

'*Que diablos!*' He could no longer stem the tide of anger. Right that moment, he wanted nothing more than to track down her bastard of a father and drive his fist into the man's face. 'They didn't take it further than just noticing, did they?'

The longer she stayed silent, the harder his breathing got.

Ignoring the pain throbbing in his groin and hip, he hauled himself against the headboard and dragged her up. Tilting her jaw, he forced her to look into his eyes. 'Did they?'

Her lower lip trembled. 'One of them did. One day after a party, I thought everyone had left. He…he came into my room and tried to force himself on me. I'd started training at the gym so I knew a few moves. I managed to struggle free and kicked him where it hurt most.'

He passed his thumb over her lips until they stopped trembling. '*Bueno*. Good girl.'

'I ran out of my room. My father was waiting in the hallway. I thought he was coming to help me because he'd heard me scream. But he wasn't…'

Rafael's blood ran cold. 'What was he doing?'

'He knew exactly why his friend had come to my room. In fact, I don't think his friend could've found my room without help.' She shuddered and goose bumps raced over her arms. He pulled her close and wrapped his arms around her.

'Did you report it to the authorities?' he asked.

She shook her head. 'I'd reported him a few times in the past and been ignored. I knew once again it would be his word against mine. I bought a baseball bat and slept with it under my pillow instead and I moved out on my eighteenth birthday.'

'Where is he now?' He entertained thoughts of tracking down the bastard, wielding his own baseball bat.

'I hadn't spoken to him until I called him last year to help my mother but, the last I heard, he'd lost all his money in some Ponzi scheme and is living with his mistress somewhere in Scotland.'

Rafael filed that piece of information away. When she gave another shudder, he kissed her again, a little deeper this time. He made sure when she shuddered again minutes later it was with a different reaction, one that set his blood singing again.

On impulse, he got out of bed and tugged her upright.

'What are you doing?' she asked.

He went into his dressing room and came out with a dark blue T-shirt. 'Put that on.'

'Why? Where are we going?'

'You'll find out in a minute.' He pulled on his shorts and grabbed her hand.

Five minutes later, she pulled at his grip. 'No, I'm not going on there.' She dug her feet into the sand when he would've tumbled her onto the wide beach bed.

'Of course you are. You've been dying to try it since we

got here.' He set down the vintage champagne and flutes he'd grabbed from the kitchen.

'Rafael, it's the middle of the night,' she protested, although her glance slid to the white-canopied bed that gleamed under the moon and starlit night.

'Where's your sense of adventure?'

'Back upstairs, where it doesn't run the risk of being eaten by sharks.'

He let go of her hand and started uncorking the champagne. 'Unless sharks have developed a way of walking on sand, you'll have to come up with a better excuse.'

'I'm not wearing any knickers. I don't want to catch cold.'

His grin was utterly shameless. 'That's a very good reason.' He popped the cork, poured out a glass of golden liquid and handed it to her. Setting the bottle down, he shucked off his shorts and got onto the bed. Casting her a hot glance, he patted the space beside him. 'I'll be your body blanket. If I fail completely in my task you'll be free to return to the safety of my bed.'

He saw her battle for a response. But his insistent patting finally won through. The mixture of hunger, innocence and vulnerability on her face touched a part of him he'd long thought dead. When she set her glass down and slid into his arms, Rafael swore to make her forget everything about her bastard of a father. If only for a few hours.

Why taking on that task meant so much to him, he refused to consider.

He made love to her with a slow, leisurely tempo even though everything inside him clamoured for quick, fiery satisfaction.

When she came apart in his arms, he let himself be swept away into his own release. Sleep wasn't far behind and, gathering her close, he kissed her temple and pulled the cashmere blanket over them.

CHAPTER TEN

THE INTRUSION OF light behind her eyelids came with firm, warm lips brushing her jaw.

'Wake up, *querida*…'

'Hmm, no…don't want to…'

A soft deep laugh. 'Come on, wake up or you'll miss the sunrise.'

'Sun…no…' She wanted to stay just as she was, suspended between dream and reality, entranced by the sultry air on her face and hard, firm…aroused male curved around her.

'Open your eyes. I promise you, it's spectacular.'

She opened her eyes, simply because she couldn't resist him, and found herself gazing into deep blue eyes. Eyes she'd looked into many times. But still her heart caught as if it'd been tugged by a powerful string.

'*Buenos dias*,' Rafael murmured. 'Look.' He nodded beyond the canopy to the east. She followed his gaze and froze at the sheer beauty of the gathering sunrise. Orange, yellow and blue where the light faded, it was nature at its most spectacular and she lay there, enfolded in Rafael's arms, silent and in complete awe as the sun spread its stunning rays across the sky.

'Wow,' she whispered.

'Indeed. Does that win me Brownie points?' he whispered hotly into her ear.

Turning from the sight, she looked again into mesmerising eyes. And once again she felt her heart stutter in awe.

'It depends what you intend to use the points for.'

'To get you to come yachting with me today. My yacht is moored at the Marina. We can take her out for the day.'

More alone time with Rafael. *Too much…too much…*

She should've heeded the screeching voice of caution. But

Raven had a feeling she was already too far gone. 'I'd love to. On one condition.'

He mock frowned. '*Condition*...my second least favourite word.'

'What's your least favourite?'

'*No.*'

She laughed. 'That figures. Well, I need to exercise. Then *you* need to have your session. Then we'll go yachting.'

With a quick, hard kiss, he released her and sat back. 'You can do your exercise right here on the beach.'

She felt heat rise. 'While you watch?'

'I'm a harmless audience. Besides, I want to see if this Krav Maga is worth all the hype.'

She bit her lip and hesitated.

'What?' he demanded.

'I...I'm not wearing any knickers, remember?'

His laugh was shameless and filled with predatory anticipation. 'Kinky Krav Maga...sounds even better.' He lounged back against the plump pillows, folded golden muscled arms and waited.

It was the hottest, most erotic exercise routine Raven had ever performed.

The rest of the day went like a dream. Rafael's yacht was the last word in luxury. With a crew of four, they sailed around the Los Cabos islands, stopped at a seafront restaurant for a lunch of cerviche and sweet potato fries, then sunbathed on the twenty-foot deck until it got too hot. Then he encouraged her to join him in the shower below deck.

She clung to him in the aftermath of another pulse-destroying orgasm.

'Hmm...I have a feeling you won't be needing my services for much longer.'

He raised his head from where he'd been kissing her damp shoulder and stared deep into her eyes. 'What makes you say that?'

'You haven't used your cane all day, and your…um…stamina seems to be endless.'

His frown was immediate, edged with tension that seeped into the atmosphere. 'You're signed on for another three months. Don't make any plans to break the contract just yet.' He moved away and grabbed two towels. He handed her one and wrapped the other around her waist, his movements jerky.

'I wasn't making plans. I was just commenting that your movements are a little more fluid. And you haven't used the cane all day today. I think it's a great sign. You should be pleased.'

'Should I?'

His icy tone made alarm skitter over her. 'What's the matter?'

He smoothed a hand over the steamed up mirror and met her gaze over his shoulder. 'Why should anything be wrong?'

'I've just given you the equivalent of an almost clean bill of health. You're reacting as if I've just told you your puppy has died.'

He whirled to face her. 'This clean bill of health, will it pass the X1 training board and see me reinstated as a race driver?'

Her breath caught. 'You're thinking of going back to racing?'

'You sound surprised.'

She licked her lips. 'Well, I am. I thought since Marco had sold the team, and Sasha had quit—'

'What are you saying, that I should follow the family tradition and quit while I'm ahead?'

'No…but—'

'You don't think I can hack it?'

'Stop putting words in my mouth, Rafael. You're almost done with phase three of the physio regime. I'm just trying to find out what your plans are so I can work with you to achieve them.'

He stalked to where she stood and gripped her nape in a

firm hold. His kiss was hot, ravaging and rage-tinged. 'Right now, my only plan is to be inside you again.'

She barely stopped herself from dissolving into a puddle of need. 'And afterwards? We can't stay here indefinitely, indulging in wall-to-wall shagging.'

His eyes narrowed, his grip tightening. 'Are you trying to set a time limit on what's happening between us? Is that what all this is about?'

The shard of steel that lodged in her chest made her breath catch. 'I don't know what you mean.'

'Don't you? From the start you've tried to manage what was happening between us, tried to define it into something you can deal with. Now you want to set a time limit on it so you can walk away once the time comes, *si*?'

'Are you saying you're not? Am I not just one more challenge to you? Can we please not delude ourselves into thinking this is anything more than sex?'

He sucked in a breath as if he'd been punched. Stepping back, he dropped his hand and left the bathroom.

Raven trailed after him into the large, exquisite gold and cream cabin. He was pulling on a pair of boxers, which he followed with cargo shorts and a white T-shirt.

Feeling exposed, she slipped on her underwear and the lilac flowered slip dress she'd worn to go sailing. 'I'm not sure what's going on here, Rafael. Or why you're annoyed with me. I may not know the rules of this sleeping together thing but even I know there is a time limit when it comes to your affairs—'

'*Affairs*? Is that what we're doing, having an affair?' he asked with a cocked eyebrow. 'How quaint.'

'Will you please stop mocking me and tell me what's really bothering you?'

He slammed the drawer he'd just opened none too gently. 'I don't like time limits. I don't being head-shrunk. And I don't like the woman I'm sleeping with hinting that she'll be leaving me the day after we start sleeping together. There, does that sum things up for you?'

'So you want to be the one to call the shots? To dictate when this aff...*liaison* starts and ends?'

He dragged a hand through his damp hair and glared at her. '*Santo cielo*, why are we even having this argument?' he shouted.

'I have no idea but you started it!' she yelled back.

His eyes widened at her tone, then he sighed. 'Forgive me, I'm used to having things my way, *pequeña*. You have every right to shout at me when I step out of line.'

'Thanks, I will.'

He laughed, and just like that the tension broke. Striding to her, he tugged her into his arms and proceeded to kiss the fight out of both of them. They sailed back to the villa shortly after and, once again, she let him coax her into spending part of the night on the beach bed.

They were halfway through their breakfast when the delivery arrived.

'What is it?'

'I've got something for you.' The gleam in his eyes was pure wickedness. Her heartbeat escalated as she eyed the large gold-ribboned package sitting on the floor beside their breakfast table.

'Don't worry, you'll enjoy it,' he promised with a smile so sexy, and so deliciously decadent, her toes curled.

Even though the subject quickly changed to their plans for the rest of the day, Raven's gaze strayed time and again to the package. But Rafael, as she'd discovered in the past two nights, was skilled in delayed gratification. He was also skilled in being the perfect host. She was stunned when she discovered how many details he'd picked up through their conversation. When he shepherded her towards the SUV mid-morning, she gaped in surprise when she found out he'd organised the hang-gliding trip she'd casually mentioned was on her list of things to do.

She'd barely descended from that high when he whisked her by helicopter to the Mayan encampment she'd been dying to explore.

'You're seriously scaring me now by how utterly close I am to adoring you for this,' she said in hushed tones as they were ushered into the hallowed grounds of the ancient burial site.

His breath hissed out. When she glanced at him, he'd paled a little.

'Rafael? Are you in pain?' He'd left his walking stick back at the villa and nothing from his gait told her he'd suffered a mishap. All the same...

He shook his head. A second later the look had disappeared. 'It's nothing.'

She stopped as the full import of her words struck her. Wide-eyed, she turned to him. 'No, I didn't mean...I was only joking...'

'Were you?' The intensity of his gaze pinned her where she stood.

'Yes! Ignore me, I'm babbling because you've made two dreams come true today.'

'So you don't adore me?'

She opened her mouth to refute the comment and found she couldn't speak. Because she realised she did adore him, and more than a little. The Rafael she'd come to know in the past few weeks had a depth she'd never got the chance to explore last year. She felt a connection to this Rafael, and not just because he'd been her first lover.

The depth of the feeling rampaging through her made her shake her head.

One corner of his mouth lifted in a mirthless smile. Then he nodded to the tour guide looking their way.

'Now that we've established that you *don't* adore me, I think you need to go see your artefacts.'

She felt a stab of disappointment. 'Aren't you coming?'

'Been there, done that.' He pulled the phone from his pocket. 'The drivers and cars arrive this afternoon. I need to return a few calls.' He walked away before she could reply.

Disappointment morphed into something else. Something she couldn't put her finger on but which confused the hell out of her. The more she tried to grasp it, the further away it slithered from her.

He was waiting when she finally emerged. Back in the helicopter, he pulled her close and sealed his lips over hers, his mouth hungry and demanding.

She was breathless when he finally pulled away. 'What was that for?' she asked huskily.

His lids swept down over his eyes. 'Maybe I want you to adore me, just a little.'

Rafael watched her breath catch all over again and wondered just what the hell he was doing. Why he was letting the angst riding underneath his skin get to him.

So she didn't adore him. Big deal. There were thousands of women out there who were more than willing to fall into his bed should he wish them to.

But none like the woman in his arms. None like the woman who refused to mould into a being he understood, could predict. Most women would be halfway to falling in love with him by now; would be secretly or not so secretly making plans on how to prolong their presence in his life.

When he wasn't kissing her breathless—a diversionary tactic he'd grown to enjoy immensely—Raven seemed to be counting the days, hell, the minutes until she could walk away from him.

The notion unsettled him enough to make him want to probe, to find an answer.

Had she glimpsed the darkness in his soul? Had opening up to her in Monaco and again in Monza made him into a man she could sleep with but not a man she wanted in her life for the long-term?

The long-term? Santa María. Had he finally lost all common sense? Certainly, reality had slid back these past two days. Being with her had been like living some sort of dream. A dream where he could look at himself in the mirror without being revolted by what stared back at him.

A dream where he could continue the secret writing project he'd started before his accident without feeling as if he was tainting the very memory he wanted to preserve.

He stared down into her face, a face flushed with pleasure from the activities of the day or, he thought semi-cockily, from kissing him. All at once he wanted to blurt his very innermost secret to her.

He stopped himself just in time.

Permanent wasn't part of his vocabulary. He wasn't about to seek it out now. And, really, he should thank his lucky stars because Raven knew his flaws and had adequately cautioned herself against getting too close.

So why did the thought not please him?

His phone rang and he happily abandoned the questions that threatened to flood him. But he didn't abandon his hold on the soft body of the woman next to him. Delight curled in his chest when she slid closer.

'De Cervantes,' he answered.

The conversation was short and succinct. And it raised every single hair on his nape to full, electrifying attention. Feeling slightly numb, he ended the call.

'What's happened?' she asked.

'One of the drivers has pulled out of the remaining races.'

'Can they do that, pull out without warning?'

He shook his head. 'I've never had a driver pull out before. Normally I have them begging to race.' She didn't miss the frown in his voice. 'But he's just been offered a race seat for the coming season and it's an opportunity of a lifetime. I recognise how important that is to a young driver.'

'So what does that mean for your event?' she asked, pulling back to stare up into his face.

He looked down but didn't really see her. The thoughts tumbling through his head both terrified and excited him at the same time.

'They can find a replacement if they search hard enough...'

Raven pulled away further. He wanted to tug her back but he couldn't seem to summon the strength it took because of the feelings rushing through him.

'Or?'

'Or...the general consensus is that I should step in.'

'No,' she said. Naked fear pulsed through the single word.

He finally focused on her, felt a burn in his stomach from the impact of her searing look. 'No?'

'You're not ready.'

'Shouldn't *I* be the judge of that? And didn't you say yourself I was almost healed?' he asked.

'Yes, *almost!* As your physiotherapist, I strongly do not recommend it. You could reverse everything you've achieved in the last several weeks...'

'If I crash?'

She paled a little, and he felt a tug of guilt for pushing her. 'I won't answer that. What I will say is that you're the head of X1 Premier Management. All you need to do is make a single phone call and any one of dozens of drivers will fly out and take your driver's place. You don't have to do this. *Please don't do it.*'

The naked plea in her eyes struck deep. The unsettling angst of a moment before subsided as he traced his finger down her face.

'Dare I believe that you care about me, just a little bit?' He couldn't stop the question from spilling out. But, once it was out there, he *needed* to know.

'I care, Rafael. More than a little bit, I think.' The naked truth struck them both. Their eyes met, locked.

Breaths held until the banking helicopter jolted them. The sight of the villa sprawled beneath them made Rafael want to swear. Instead he activated his phone again.

'Angelo—' he addressed his second-in-command '—call around the teams, find out if there's any driver who isn't testing and offer them a place on the newly available seat on the All-Star event. You know which guys I rate the most. Tell them they're guaranteed a spread in the next issue of *X1 Magazine* and my personal endorsement of whatever charity they choose. Oh, and I want a driver on his way to the racetrack in Los Cabos by the end of the day.' He ended the call and looked down at her.

'Now what?' he asked softly as the helicopter blades slowed to a halt.

Her smile held such radiance he found it hard to breathe. 'Now, I may let myself adore you a little bit more…see where it takes me.'

He regretted that he wasn't healed enough to swing her into his arms and carry her off to his lair. But he was well enough to drag her from the helicopter to his bedroom. And he made sure he kept her fully occupied until neither of them could move.

'You never told me what was in the package,' Raven murmured, drifting somewhere between *I-can't-move* satiation and a drugging need to experience that mind-bending pleasure all over again.

The wicked grin he sent her way made her heart pound all over again. He left the bed and she could no more help herself from visually devouring him than she could stop breathing.

He picked up the package from the foot of the bed and returned it to her. 'This may just buy me a few more Brownie points.'

That got her attention. She dragged herself up to lean on one elbow. The sight of his naked chest threatened to fry her brain cells. 'What is it?' Her mind whirled with the possibilities, then latched onto what she wanted it to be. Could it be the rest of his manuscript?

Her senses now on a high, she stared down at the box,

feeling like a kid on Christmas morning. 'What's in the box, Rafael?'

He lifted the lid. All she could see were sheaves of wrapping paper. 'See for yourself.'

Carefully, she lifted the sheer paper. The first items made her heart knock in her chest. And not in a good way. Praying she was dreaming, she nudged the material aside with her finger and looked underneath. Each layer held more of the same.

'Naughty underwear? *That's* what you got me?' Raven let the garments drop back into the box, unable to stem the cold wave of hurt that washed over her. She wasn't even sure why it hurt so much. But it felt as if she'd climbed a mountain only to look back and find out that she'd only taken a few steps.

He looked genuinely stunned. 'You don't like it?'

'What's wrong with my own underwear?'

His perplexed look deepened. For the first time, Rafael looked seriously nonplussed. It would have been funny had it not been so far from funny.

'I didn't…I just wanted to…' He stopped, a flush lighting his high cheekbones.

If someone had told her as little as a week ago that she'd be sitting in bed discussing naughty lingerie with Rafael, she'd have laughed herself blind.

Now, she forced herself to glance at the lacy silks and delicate satin bows that didn't seem as if they would stand up to any overt pressure.

'That's not even my size, Rafael. I'm a size twelve, remember?'

His flush deepened. 'I have a feeling you'll punch me when I tell you I don't have a clue what size underwear you wear or what yours look like. By the time I get to your panties, I'm nearly insane with lust. Damn it. I've got it spectacularly wrong, haven't I?'

'Not all wrong. You got my favourite colours right.'

He picked up the package and flung it across the room.

Then he tugged her close. 'Is there any way I can make you forget the last ten minutes?'

Against her will and certainly against her better judgement, she glanced at the lilac silk material caught over a chair back. It seemed so delicate and forlorn.

'I don't need expensive lingerie to feel sexy. If you don't want me as I am—'

He caught her chin between his fingers. 'I do,' he breathed. 'Let me prove it…' His head started to descend.

Raven's gaze swung once more to the basque. Pulling herself from his arms, she walked, naked, to the garment and plucked it off the chair. Carefully, she rubbed the material between her fingers and turned. Rafael's breath caught as she slowly traced the warm silk over her body.

A glance from beneath her lashes showed a definite effect on him.

Pure feminine power washed away her misgivings. With a wanton smile she'd never have believed herself capable of, she sauntered back towards him.

'You need to understand one thing, Rafael.'

He nodded but his eyes were riveted on her breasts. '*Sí?*'

'You promise never to buy me lingerie again as long as we're together. I choose my own underwear.'

He swallowed and nodded.

Raven glanced down at the panties and shook her head. 'I can't believe you thought I was a size eight,' she muttered.

'*Por favor!* Forgive me.' He wet his lips in such a blatantly sexual way, a blush suffused her whole body.

'You're just saying that so I hurry back to bed.'

'*Sí.* And you can forget the lingerie if you wish.'

'And give up the chance to see you sweat. No can do.' She slowly, deliberately swept her hair to one side before sliding the lace-trimmed garment over her head.

She nearly bottled it then, but the scorching intensity in his eyes had the direct effect of firing up her courage. The soft lilac tulle basque hugged her breasts in such a blatant caress, she bit her lower lip to stop a moan of excitement. She turned, then glanced back over her shoulder.

'Are you going to help me with the laces?' she rasped.

'*Dios mío*, what are you trying to do?'

'Teach you a lesson.'

He got off the bed, almost a little too eager for his punishment. 'Turn around,' he instructed.

She did, and heard him hiss out a breath as he pulled the delicate laces and tied it.

'Once again, I have no knickers.'

His moan was a heartfelt balm to her soul.

Turning, she placed her hands on her hips, feminine power fuelling her desire as she saw her effect on him.

When he stumbled back and sank onto the side of the bed, she laughed. 'Hoisted by your own petard, Rafael?'

She took a step towards him and gloried in the slide of the silk on her skin. She would never don anything like this again. Naughty lingerie wasn't really her style but, just for tonight, she would allow herself this experience.

His face was strained like the steely erection that jutted from between his legs. Heat oozed between her thighs, made her movements slow as the magnetic force between them pulled her inexorably into his orbit.

When she reached him, she raked her fingers down his chest. 'You won't see me like this again, Rafael, so look your fill.'

His features altered, a look of regret passing through his eyes that made her stomach hollow out. 'You're breathtaking without it, Raven. How can I make this up to you?'

Her heart thundered at the sincerity in his voice. 'You don't need to. Just see me as I am.'

He inhaled, long and deep, and dropped his head between her breasts. For a long moment, Raven held him close. Then his breathing altered. Hers followed as lust sizzled, rose to the fore once more.

She pushed him back on the bed and climbed on top of him. By the time he donned the condom, they were both nearly insane with need. She'd barely positioned her thighs on either side of him when he thrust hard and deep inside her. Raven lost all coherent thought.

In the sizzling, excruciatingly heady aftermath, she curled into him but found she couldn't breathe, even after his deft fingers pulled the basque from her body and flung it away. She'd always known that Rafael's dominance was larger than life. But she'd trusted herself not to get pulled into his devastating, fast-spinning orbit. Her emotions were fast skittering out of control. How long had she watched her mother experience the same devastation over and over? Now she was running the same risk—

'What is it?' he demanded, his intuitiveness almost scary.

'Nothing…' she started to say, then stopped. 'How many times have you done this?' she blurted.

'I think I definitely need a definition of *this,* otherwise I'll have to plead the fifth.'

'Bought risqué underwear for a woman?'

His lids dropped for a second before rising to spear her with that intense blue. 'Never.'

Her snort was borne of disbelief and a sharp pang she didn't want to touch with a dozen bargepoles. She shook her head and started to move away.

He caught her back easily. A shiver ran through her when his finger slid under her chin and tilted her head up. Almost afraid, she looked into his eyes.

'I've never lied to you, Raven. I'm skilled in evading subjects I don't wish to discuss, but I have never and will never lie to you. Understood?'

She was stunned by how much she wanted to believe him, how much she wanted to be the first at something in his life. 'Why haven't you done this before?'

Surprise flared in his eyes. 'You're asking me why I haven't bought lingerie for a woman before?'

She pursed her lips. 'It seems the kind of thing ruthless playboys specialise in.'

His own lips flattened at the label, then he shrugged and relaxed onto the pillows. 'Not specialise. I have knowledge of it because I'm always the recipient. The assumption has always been that I would prefer the bedroom unveiling to be a knock-my-brains-out surprise, not a joint enterprise. I haven't felt the inclination to alter that assumption.'

A small fizz of pleasure started in her belly. Which was really foolish because she knew this particular experiment had been a means to an end for him.

Unwilling to face up to what all this meant, she buried her face in his neck. 'I'm glad.'

'Enough to forgive my grievous error?'

'That depends.'

'On?'

'On whether you'll give me what I expected to find in the box when I opened it.' She told him.

Another peculiar look crossed his face. 'The story has reached a crossroads.'

'Are you saying I did all of that for nothing?'

He pushed her firmly onto her back and leaned his powerful, endlessly intoxicating body over hers. Unable to resist, she let her hands wander at will over smooth muscle.

'For nothing? No, *bonita*, it was most definitely not for nothing. I think you could be the key to unlocking everything.'

Although she went into his arms at his urging, Raven sensed he wasn't as in control as he made out. She'd heard a different note in his voice—part vulnerability, part bravado. She slid her hand up and down his back in a strong need to comfort him. The persistent voice that had cautioned against getting too deep was receding—almost as if it knew the path she'd chosen. She would live in this fantasy now.

This magic, this overwhelming sense that she was exactly

where she wanted to be, was too great to deny. Reality would encroach soon enough.

So where was the harm in experiencing it for a little while longer?

CHAPTER ELEVEN

It turned out a little while was all she would get.

Things started to go wrong the moment the helicopter touched down at the Autódromo Hermanos Rodríguez in Mexico City the next morning. The replacement driver Angelo had lined up didn't turn up. As the day went on with no immediate solution, Raven felt the pressure mount as everyone turned to Rafael for a solution.

Even though this was primarily a charity event, high profile sponsors had channelled millions of euros into it in the hope of gaining maximum exposure, courtesy of the sold-out events. Racing five cars instead of the usual six would make the headlines and throw negative publicity on the event—something X1 Premier Management and Rafael in particular couldn't afford to let happen.

Already the paparazzi, sensing blood in the water, were sniffing around, cameras and microphones poised to capture any salacious gossip.

She recalled how they'd decimated Sasha de Cervantes and her gut churned at the thought of what that type of publicity could do to Rafael.

As if she'd conjured him up, Rafael walked past the window, his pace carrying him from one end of the air-conditioned VIP lounge to the other, his gait remarkably improved despite the physical stress she'd put on his body in the last three days.

Feeling a blush creep up her face, she glanced away before he or any of the other management team hastily assembled for the meeting could guess at her thoughts.

Angelo, Rafael's assistant, approached him, a phone in his

hand. Rafael listened for several seconds, his tension increasing with each breath he took.

'Tell him if he threatens me with a lawsuit one more time, I'll personally see to it that his brand of vodka never leaves the icy wilderness of Siberia...*bueno*, I'm pleased you're finally seeing things my way. We will find a driver, and your logo will be emblazoned on the side pod just as we agreed.'

He hung up, glanced around the room and caught a few nervous gazes. 'They want to play dirty; I'm more than happy to oblige.'

A three-time world champion, now in his early sixties, cleared his throat. 'The race starts in three hours. I don't see that we have much of a choice here. You all but agreed to step in two days ago when we were a driver short. I'm not sure what changed your mind but perhaps you'd revisit the idea of racing?'

Raven half rose out of her seat, the scrape of her chair on the tiled floor drawing attention from the rest of the room.

She collapsed back into her seat when Rafael's fierce gaze settled on her. When the quick shake of her head didn't seem to register, she cleared her throat.

His eyes narrowed. Then he turned, slowly, deliberately away from her.

A block of ice wedged in her chest and her stomach hollowed out. From very far away, she heard him address the race coordinator and chief engineer of the driverless team.

'I have a couple of spare seats around here somewhere. Angelo will arrange to supply you with one to fit into the car. I'll be along in ten minutes to go over race strategy with you.' He looked around the room, the devil's own grin spreading over his face. 'Gentlemen, let's go racing.'

The explosion of excitement that burst through the room drowned out her horrified gasp. Manly slaps of his shoulder and offers of congratulations echoed through her numb senses.

When someone suggested a quick press conference, Raven

finally found the strength to stand and approach him as the room emptied.

'R...Rafael, can I talk to you?'

'Now is not a good time, *bonita*.' His voice was brusque to the point of rudeness.

The endearment she was beginning to adore suddenly grated. But she refused to be dismissed. 'I think this is a bad idea.'

'*Sí*, I knew you would think so. But I can't help what you think. Needs must and I stand to become embroiled in all sorts of legal wrangling if this isn't sorted out.'

She frowned. 'But it was the driver who broke the contract. Isn't he liable?'

'No, he isn't. XPM is staging this event, so I'm responsible. I should've taken more time to ensure contingencies were in place before we arrived. Everyone here knows someone's dropped the ball. Unfortunately, they're looking at me to pick it up and run with it.' He was the hard businessman, the ruthless racer who'd held a finite edge over his competitors for years.

He was certainly nothing like the lover who'd taken her to the heights of ecstasy.

She fought to regain her own professionalism, to put aside the hurt splintering her insides. 'As your physiotherapist, I'll have to recommend that you don't race.'

'Your recommendation is duly noted. Is that all?'

Her fists clenched in futile anger. Anger she wanted to let loose but couldn't. Her days of lashing out were far, far behind her. 'No, that's not all! This is crazy. You're risking your health, not to mention your life, Rafael.'

His smile was tight and tension-filled. 'And *you* are running the risk of overstepping, *querida*. I won't be tacky enough to point out just what your role is in my life considering the lines have been blurred somewhat, but I expect you to recognise the proper time and place for voicing disagreement.'

The blunt words hit her like a slap in the face. Regret momentarily tightened his face, then it smoothed once again into the outward mask of almost bored indifference.

It took every ounce of self-control to contain her composure. 'No, you're right. Pardon me for thinking of your health first.' She indicated the frenzy outside, the racetrack and the baking heat under which the cars gleamed. 'Off you go, then. And good luck.'

He reached forward and grabbed her arm when she'd have turned away.

'Aren't you forgetting something?'

'What?' She made herself look into his eyes, determined not to be cowed by the storm of fear rolling through her gut. He returned her look with one that momentarily confused her. Had her thoughts been clearer, Raven would've sworn Rafael was scared out of his wits.

'As my physio, you need to come with me, attend to my needs until I'm in the cockpit. Have you forgotten your role already?'

She had. Whether intentionally or through mental blockage, she'd tried to put her role eight months ago as Rafael's race physio out of her mind. Because every time she thought of it, she remembered their last row. Her rash, heated words; the stunned look on his face as he'd absorbed her bone-stripping insults before he'd walked out to his car. They'd been in a situation like this, momentarily alone in a place that buzzed with suppressed energy. His race suit had been open and around his neck she'd spied his customary chain with the cross on it. The cross he kissed before each race.

In the months since, she'd remembered vividly that Rafael hadn't kissed his cross that day…

Now, Raven was in favour of forgetting all about it. All she wanted to do right now was find a dark corner, stay there and not come out until the blasted race was over. Watching his crash that day had been one of the most heart-wrenching experiences of her life. She would give anything not to be put in that position again.

But she had a job to do. Sucking a sustaining breath, she nodded. 'Of course, whatever you need.' Pulling herself from his grasp, she walked towards the bar and picked up two bottles of mineral water. She handed him one. 'We're a little late off the mark in trying to hydrate you sufficiently so I'd suggest you get as much liquid in as possible.'

He took the bottle from her but made no move to drink the water.

'You think I'm making the wrong decision.' It wasn't a question.

'What I think is no longer relevant, remember?' Her gaze dropped meaningfully to the bottle.

He uncapped it and drank without taking his gaze off her face. She felt the heavy force of his stare but studiously avoided eye contact. When he finished and tossed the empty bottle aside, she handed him the second bottle.

'Drink this one in about ten minutes.' She started to walk towards the door, eager to get away from the clamouring need to throw herself in his path, to stop him putting himself in any danger.

Too late, she realised the media had camped outside the door, eager to jump on the latest news of Rafael's return.

Is this the start of your comeback?

Are you sure you can take the pressure?

Which team will you be driving for when the X1 season starts next month?

Rafael fielded their questions without breaking a sweat, all the while keeping a firm hold on her elbow. Every time she tried to free herself, he held on tighter.

Raven spotted the keen reporter from the corner of her eye.

Is there a new woman in your life?

Without the barest hint of affront, he smiled. 'If I told you that you'd stop hounding me, then my life would no longer be worth living, would it?'

The paparazzi, normally a vicious thrill-seeking lot, actually laughed. Raven marvelled at the spectacle. Then berated herself for failing to realise the obvious. Sooner or later, everyone, man, woman or child, fell under Rafael's uniquely enthralling spell.

She'd fooled herself into believing she could fall only a little, that she could go only so far before, wisely and safely, she pulled back from the dizzying precipice.

How wrong she'd been. Wasn't she right now experiencing the very depths of hell because she couldn't stand the thought of him being hurt again?

Hadn't she spent half the night awake, her stomach tied in knots as she'd wondered why so beautiful a man suffered tortured dreams because of his choices and his determination to shut everyone out?

She hadn't missed the phone calls from his father that he'd avoided, or the one from Marco yesterday that he'd swiftly ended when she entered the room.

Pain stabbed deep as she acknowledged that she'd come to adore him just a little bit more than she'd planned to. She'd probably started adoring him the moment he'd answered her call and agreed to see her in Barcelona seven weeks ago.

Because by allowing her in just that little bit meant he didn't hate her as much as he should. Or maybe he didn't hate her at all.

Or maybe she was deluding herself.

'A three-line frown. Stop it or I'll have to do something drastic, like confirm to them just who the new woman in my life is. Personally, I don't mind drastic but I have a feeling you wouldn't enjoy being eaten alive by the paparazzi.'

She'd been walking alongside him without conscious thought as to where they were going. The sound of the engine revving made her jump. 'No, I wouldn't.'

'*Bueno*, then behave.'

They'd arrived at the garage of the defected racer. Rafael grabbed the nearest sound-cancelling headphones and passed them to her.

She was about to put them on when she spotted Chantilly,

lounging with a bored look on her face on the other side of the garage. The second she spotted Rafael, she came to vivacious life.

'Damn it, your frown just deepened. What did I say about behaving?'

'What's she doing here? In this garage, I mean?'

Rafael followed her gaze to Chantilly, then glanced back at her. 'Her husband owns this team.'

The single swear word escaped before she could stop it. A slow grin spread over Rafael's face but it didn't pack the same charismatic punch as it usually did. Examining him closer, she noted the lines of strain around his mouth.

'Sheath your claws, *chiquita*. I told you, I have no interest in her. Not after discovering the delights of fresh English roses.' A pulse of heat from his eyes calmed her somewhat but it was gone far too quickly for her to feel its warmth.

The chief engineer called out for Rafael and, with another haunted look down at her, he went over to discuss telemetry reports with the team.

The ninety minutes before the race passed with excruciating slowness. With every second that counted down, Raven's insides knotted harder. The walk across the sun-baked pit lane into the race lane felt like walking the most terrifying gauntlet.

She hitched the emergency bag higher on her shoulder and took her place beside Rafael's car, making sure to keep the umbrella above his head to protect his suit-clad body from overheating. She ignored the sweat trickling down her own back to check for signs of distress on him.

'If you feel your hip tightening, try those pelvic rotations we practised by flexing your spine. I know you don't have much room in the cockpit but give it a try anyway,' she said, trying desperately to hang on to a modicum of professionalism.

He nodded but didn't look up. His attention was fixed on the dials on his steering wheel. When the first red light flashed on, signalling it was time to clear the track, Raven opened her mouth to say something…anything, but her throat had closed up.

She took one step back, and another.

'Rafael…' she whispered.

His head swung towards her, ice-blue eyes capturing hers for a single naked second.

The stark emptiness in his eyes made her heart freeze over.

Rafael fought to regulate his breathing. Shards of memories pierced his mind, drenching his spine and palms in cold sweat.

His fight with Marco the night before the Hungary race…

You're dishonouring Mamá's memory by continuing with this reckless behaviour…

Sasha's voice joined the clamouring…*it's not okay for you to let everyone think you're a bastard.*

And Raven's condemning truth…*you're a useless waste of space…who cares about nothing but himself and his own vacuous pleasures…*

He tried to clear his mind but he knew it wouldn't be that easy. Those words had carried him into that near fatal corner that day in Hungary because he'd known they all spoke the truth. What they hadn't known was that the day had held another meaning for him. It was emblazoned into his memory like a hot iron brand.

That day in Hungary had been exactly eight years to the day he'd charmed his mother into the ride that had ended her life…the day he'd let partying too hard snuff out a life he'd now happily give his own to have returned.

Looking into Raven's eyes just now, he'd known she was recalling her words, too; he'd seen the naked fear and remorse in her eyes. But he hadn't been able to offer reassurance.

How could he, when he knew deep down she was right? Since his mother's death, he'd lived in the special place in hell he'd reserved for himself. That *no trespassing* place where no one and nothing was allowed to touch him.

It was a place he planned on staying…

No matter how horrifyingly lonely…

His gaze darted to the lights as they lit up. Jaw tight, he tried to empty his mind of all thought, but her face kept intruding…her pleading eyes boring into his ravaged soul despite every effort to block her out.

Que diablos!

He stepped on the accelerator a touch later than he'd planned and cursed again as Axel Jung and Matteo, the teenage driver, shot past him on either side. Even in a showcase event like this one, a fraction of a second was all it took to fall behind.

Adrenaline and age-old reflexes kicked in but Rafael knew he was already at a disadvantage. He eyed the gap to the right on the second corner, and calculated that he could slot himself in there if he was quick enough. He pressed his foot down and felt his pulse jump when Axel, in a bid to cut him off, positioned himself in front of him.

In a move he'd perfected long before he'd been tall enough to fit into an X1 cockpit, he flicked his wrist and dashed down the left side of the track. Too late, Axel tried to cover his mistake but Rafael was already a nose ahead of the German. From the corner of his eye, he saw the other driver flick him a dirty gesture.

Where normally he'd have grinned with delight behind his helmet, Rafael merely gestured back and pressed down even harder on the accelerator, desperately trying to outrun his demons the way he had that day in Hungary.

You're not all bad…

Yes, he was. Even his father looked at him with pity and sadness.

His father…the man he'd put in a wheelchair. The man who kept calling and leaving him messages because Rafael was too afraid…too ashamed to talk to him.

The car shot forward faster. Inside his helmet, his race engineer's voice cautioned him on the upcoming bend. The words barely registered before disappearing under the heavy weight of his thoughts. He took the bend without lifting off the throttle or easing back on his speed.

He heard the muted roar of the appreciative crowd but the spark of excitement he'd expected from the recognition that he was still in fine racing form, that his accident hadn't made him lose what was most important to him, didn't manifest.

That was when the panic started.

For as long as he could recall, that excitement had been present. No matter what else was going on in his life, racing was the one thing that had always…*always* given him a thrill, given him a reason to push forward.

Fear clutched his chest as he searched for and found only emptiness. In front of him, Matteo had made a mistake that had cost him a few milliseconds, bringing Rafael into passing distance of him.

He could pass him, using the same move he'd used in Hungary. He had nothing to lose. The grin that spread over his face felt alien yet oddly calming, as did the black haze that started to wash over his eyes.

He had nothing to lose…

'Rafael, your liquid level readings show you haven't taken a drink in the last thirty minutes.'

Her voice…husky, low, and filled with fearful apprehension, shot into his head with the power of a thunderclap. He gasped as he felt himself yanked back from the edge, from the dark abyss he'd been staring into.

For a single second, he hated her for intruding.

'Rafael?'

Sucking in a breath, he glanced up and realised Matteo had regained his speed and was streaking ahead. And still, Rafael felt…nothing.

'Rafael, please respond.' A shaky plea.

He didn't, because he couldn't speak, but he took a drink and kept his foot on the pedal until the race was over.

The shoulder slaps of congratulations for coming in second washed right over him. On the podium, he smiled, congratulated Axel and even felt a little spurt of pride when Matteo took the top step, but all through it he was numb.

The moment he stepped off the podium, he ripped off his race suit. He brushed away the engineer's request for a post race analysis, his every sense shrieking warning of imminent disaster.

He rushed out of the garage, for the first time in his life ignoring the media pen, the paparazzi and news anchors who raced after him for a sound bite.

Relief rushed through him as he entered his motor home and slammed the door shut behind him.

'Rafael?'

Dios mío. Had he lost it so completely he was now hearing her voice in his head? Bile surged through his stomach and leapt into his throat. He barely made it to the bathroom before he retched with a violence that made his eyes water.

For several minutes he hunched over the bowl, feelings coursing through him that he couldn't name. No…he knew what those feelings were, it was just that he'd never allowed them room in his life.

He was a racing driver. Racing was his lifeblood. Therefore he had no room for despair or fear. He was used to success, to adrenaline-fuelled excitement. To pride and satisfaction in what he did. So why the hell was he puking his guts out while fear churned through his veins?

Because, *diablo*, he *had* finally parted ways with reality.

With a stark laugh and a shake of his head, he cleaned up after himself, rinsed his mouth thoroughly…

And turned to find Raven in the doorway, her face deathly pale and her gorgeous eyes wide with panic.

'*Madre de dios.* What the hell are you doing here?'

CHAPTER TWELVE

'ARE YOU ALL right?' Raven asked, making a small movement forward.

Rafael instinctively stepped back from her. If she touched him, she would know. And whatever else he was...*or wasn't*, the last thing he wanted Raven Blass, this infuriatingly bright, mind-bendingly sexy woman, to see was his fear.

He took another step back, feeling more exposed than he'd ever felt in his life.

The water he'd splashed over his face chilled his skin. 'Am I all right? Sure. I puke my guts out after every race. Didn't you know that?'

'No you don't.' She took another step closer and, instantly, another more urgent need surged to the fore. The need to grab her, plaster her warm, giving body against his, use her to stem the tide of icy numbness spreading over him.

Use her...

Bile threatened to rise again and he swallowed hard. He stepped past her, entered the bedroom and started to undress.

'Tell me what's wrong.'

Rafael glanced down at his hands and realised they were shaking. The realisation stunned him so completely, his whole body shuddered before he could control himself. The idea that he was losing control so completely, so unstoppably, made irrational anger whip up inside him.

'Stop it, Raven. Stop trying to save me. You've done your penance.'

'Excuse me?' Her voice was hushed but strong.

'That's what you've wanted since you phoned me up two months ago, isn't it? To hear that I forgive you for what you think you did to cause my accident?'

'What I think...' She sucked in a sharp breath. 'Are you saying you remember why you crashed?'

He firmed his lips. *Brava*, Rafael. 'Perhaps I do. Or perhaps I'm just tired of watching you fall on your sword over and over again. I wouldn't be surprised if that was why you gave me your virginity, considering you didn't like me much before then.'

He felt like the lowest form of life when her colour receded completely. But, *dios*, admiringly she rallied.

'You're trying to push me away by being hateful. But I won't leave until you tell me what happened out there today.'

'What do you mean, what happened? I raced. I came second. Considering I've been out of the game for nearly a year, I think that's a commendable start, don't you?'

He shucked his suit and peeled off the fire-retardant long-sleeved gear. Her eyes darkened but she didn't lose her determination.

'Aside from the fact that you didn't hydrate nearly enough, why did you not pass Matteo the half a dozen times you had the chance?'

'What are you talking about? After he recovered his mistake in Sector 4 there was never a chance to pass Matteo...'

'Of course there was. He damaged his front wing when he went too close to the pit wall on his exit but you stayed behind him when you could've passed. And many times you came close to passing him but you pulled back every time. Your race engineer tried to talk to you but you didn't respond.'

He froze, scrambled around to supply the adequate information to refute her words and came up blank. Panic cloaked his skin, sank its claws deeper into him.

'Are you saying you don't remember?' she almost whispered, her voice thick with emotion.

Rafael couldn't breathe. 'I...no, I don't remember.'

The black haze crowded his mind, encroaching rapidly with each excruciating second. He knew he was in deep trouble when he didn't stop her from touching him, from pulling him down to sit on the king-sized bed.

'Rafael, you're freezing. And you're shaking!'

His laugh was hollow. '*Sí*. In case you haven't guessed yet, *querida*, I'm a hot mess right now.'

'Oh God!' She threw her arms around him, her warm hands pressing into his skin.

Another series of shudders raked through him, setting his teeth chattering. Her fingers speared through his hair, pulling him down into the crook of her neck. He wanted to move, *needed* to move. But he stayed right where he was, selfishly absorbing her warmth, her heady scent, inhaling her very essence as if that would save him. But nothing could save him. He was beyond redemption in more ways than he could count.

Blanking out behind the wheel had cemented the realisation.

And still he found himself leaning into her, his lips finding that soft, sweet spot below her ear lobe where he knew she loved to be kissed. He kissed it, felt her try to shift away, and trapped her in his arms.

'Rafael…'

He trailed his mouth down her neck, to the pulse that jumped when he flicked his tongue against it.

The shaking receded a little, the numbness fading under the pulse of seductive heat that was all Raven. Greedily, he tried to grab onto it, to delay the encroaching darkness beneath the bliss of her touch. With a deep groan, he moved to cup her breasts.

Only to fall into a deeper hell when she pulled away and rushed to her feet.

'Sex isn't going to make this problem go away.'

Darkness prowled closer. 'I know, but a guy can still dream, can't he?'

'No, it's time for reality. We need to discuss what happened. When I saw you throwing up, I thought it was a panic attack. But I think it's more than that,' she said.

Ice snapped through him, freezing him once more to the soul. 'Leave it, Raven.'

'No, you need help, Rafael.'

He couldn't hold her gaze—she saw far too much—so he concentrated on his clenched fists. 'And you think you're the one to offer that help?'

He knew his tone was unduly harsh but he had gone beyond remorse. He was in his special frozen place.

'What happened?' Her voice pleaded for understanding.

Since he was at a loss himself, he contemplated silence. Then he contemplated seduction. When bile threatened, he contemplated pleading for mercy.

Through frozen lips, he found himself speaking. 'I remembered everything about the race in Hungary.'

He looked up to see her hands fly to her lips. He gave a grim smile and stared back down at his hands. Hands that shook uncontrollably.

'You know what I remember most about it?'

She shook her head.

'As I went to the wall, I knew, no matter what happened, no matter how hard I tried, I wasn't going to die.'

'You mean you…*wanted* to die?' Horror coated her words.

He shrugged. 'It doesn't matter what I wanted. I knew it wasn't going to happen. My expertise lies in many other areas. Killing myself isn't one of them.'

'I don't… Explain, please.'

He raised his head, took in her tall, proud figure and felt a moment of regret that he'd messed this up too. She was one thing he'd have fought to hang on to, if it hadn't been too late for him.

'I've been dicing with death since I was old enough to walk. If a situation has an element of danger, I'm there. Being born with racing imprinted into my DNA was just a bonus.'

'Even if it ends up consuming you so thoroughly it kills you?'

The look that came over his face was so gut-wrenchingly

stark she felt pain resonate inside her. 'Sorry, I didn't mean it like that—'

He shook his head. 'I won't die from racing.'

'Are you retiring?'

He dashed the hope in her question. 'No. Regardless of everything that's happened, I still crave it. I've been spared death so far. It seems I'm destined for other things.'

A frown formed. 'What do you mean?'

'Haven't you guessed it yet? My skill lies in killing everything I come into contact with. If you haven't woken to the fact that all I'll bring to your doorstep is utter chaos then you're not as bright as I thought.'

'That sounds like...are you trying to warn me off you?'

He laughed. '*Sí*, I am. Which in itself is strange. Normally, I just take what I want and leave the husk behind.'

Pain darkened her eyes. 'Why are you doing this?'

'Doing what, *querida*?'

'Trying to belittle what we have, and don't use that endearment any more. It's a beautiful word you've made tacky because you don't really mean it. You're trying to paint yourself in a vile light, trying to put me off you so I'll walk away.'

'I'm not *trying*. I'm telling you I'm not a great bet for you. I always escape unscathed but everyone I come into contact with sooner or later suffers for it.'

'You make yourself sound as if you've got a contagious disease. Stop it. And no one suffered today. You still need to address exactly what happened during the race but no one had an accident.'

'That's where you're wrong. At the start, when I realised I was getting squeezed out, I contemplated a move that would've taken Matteo out. For a moment, I forgot that I was supposed to be his teacher. I forgot the reason I'm staging the All-Star event in the first place. In that cockpit, I was just a racer, programmed to win.'

'But isn't that what racers do?'

'He's only nineteen, Raven! And I came within a whisker

of taking him out. Do you know his mother is here today? Can you imagine how devastated she'd have been if I'd crossed that line?'

'But you didn't cross it. You pulled back before you did any damage.'

'Yeah, and you know how I felt? Nothing. No remorse, no victory, no sympathy. I felt nothing.'

'Because there was something else going on. You say you remembered your crash in Hungary but then you blanked out the rest of the race. That could be a form of PTSD.'

He raked a hand through his hair. '*Santo cielo!* Stop trying to make excuses for me. Stop trying to make me the sort of man you'll fall for. There is nothing beneath this shell.'

Raven's heart lurched, then thundered so hard she was surprised it didn't burst out of her chest. Surprised she managed to keep breathing, to keep standing upright despite the knee-weakening realisation that it was too late.

She had fallen hard. So very, very hard for Rafael.

'And if I don't fall in with your plan to drive me away? You know me well enough by now to know I'm no pushover.'

He speared her with a vicious look meant to flay the skin from her flesh, and maybe a few weeks ago she'd have heeded the warning, but she'd found, when it came to Rafael, she was made of sterner stuff than that.

'No, but I'm a complete bastard when I'm pushed to the edge, *chiquita*. Are you prepared for that?' he parried.

'You'll have to do more than throw words at me. I *know* you, Rafael. I see beyond your so-called shell. And I know, despite what you say, you love your family and would do anything for them. I also know that you're pissed off right now because you're terrified of what's happening with you. But I'm not walking away, no matter how much you try to push me. I won't let you.'

Anger hissed through his teeth. Rising from the bed, he stalked, albeit with a barely visible limp, to the drawer that held his clothes and pulled it open. 'A few days ago, you were counting the days until this thing between us ended. Now I'm trying to end it and you've suddenly gone ostrich on me?' He returned with a handful of clothes.

'I'm not burying my head in the sand—far from it. I'm trying to understand. What have you done that's so viciously cruel that you think I'll walk away from you?'

He froze before her, his whole body stiffening into marble stillness. Only his lips moved, but even then no words emerged.

A chord of fear struck her. 'Rafael?'

'What does your mother mean to you?' he rasped.

Although she wondered at the change of subject, her answer was immediate. 'Everything. She's the only family I have. She may think I'm her enemy half the time because she doesn't want to be where she is, and she may blame me some of the time, imagining I'm the reason my father doesn't want her, but the times she's lucid, she's a wonderful human being and I love her unconditionally, regardless of what persona she is on any given day. The thought of her, safe and a phone call away, makes me happy. I'll do anything for her...' Her words drifted to nothing when she saw the look on his face. He'd grown paler with each word she'd uttered, the jeans he'd pulled from the drawer crushed in his vice-like grip. His face, hewn from a mask of pain so visceral, made her step towards him.

He stepped back swiftly, evoking a vivid image of carrying the contagion she'd accused him of seconds ago.

'Well, stay away from me, then, and enjoy that luxury. Because once you have me in your life, you may not have her for long.' His voice came from far away, as if from the shell he'd referred to moments ago.

'What on earth are you talking about?'

'You know I put my father in a wheelchair eight years ago. But, even before that, my life was on a slippery downward slope.'

'You've let yourself suffer enough. You have to learn to forgive yourself, Rafael.'

His head went back as if she'd struck him. 'Forgive myself? For not only crippling my own father but for taking away the one person he treasured the most?'

'What did you do?'

'*I killed my mother*, Raven. I put her in my car, drove too fast into a sharp corner and executed a perfect somersault that snuffed her out within minutes.'

The horror that engulfed her had nothing to do with his emotionless recounting of events. No, the dismay that rocked through her stemmed from knowing just how much more he'd suffered, how he'd buried it all under the perfect front.

His laugh was a harsh, cruel sound. 'Now that's more like it. That look of horror is what I expect. Maybe now you'll listen to me when I suggest you stay away from me.'

He pulled on his jeans, fished out a black polo shirt and shrugged into it.

Reeling as she was from the news he'd delivered, it took her a moment to realise what he was saying into his phone.

'You're leaving Mexico?' she asked when he hung up.

'The race is over. The next one isn't for another four days.'

She started in surprise. 'Where are you going?'

He gave her a grim smile. 'No. The twenty questions is over, *quer*—' He stopped, looked around, then shoved more things into the large bag he'd placed on the bed.

Scrambling wildly, she said, 'What about your physio sessions?'

'I've just endured a two-hour race. I hardly think I'm going to crumble into a million little pieces if I go without a session for a few days.'

Her lips firmed but the questions hammered in her mind. 'No, you won't. As long as you're not attempting to skydive over any volcanoes?'

'Been there, done that.'

His phone rang. He stared at it for several seconds, pain rippling in tides over his face. Finally, sucking in a deep breath, he answered it.

'*Sí*, Papá?' he rasped.

Raven's heart caught. The faint hope that help for Rafael would come from another angle was stymied when the conversation grew heated with bursts of staccato responses.

Rafael grew tenser with each passing moment until his body was as taut as a bow.

The moment he hung up, he reached for his bag. The action held an air of permanence about it that terrified her.

'So, I'll see you at the track in Rio?' she asked, hating herself for the desperation in her voice.

He gave her a smile that didn't reach his eyes. He started to answer but his phone rang again. He stared into her eyes, his expression inscrutable save for the tinge of relief she glimpsed before he masked it.

'No, you won't. *Adios, bonita.*'

He pressed the *answer* button, raised the phone to his ear and walked out of the door.

Rafael told himself to keep moving. To walk away before he brought chaos to her life. Time was running out for him.

He knew he wasn't ready to give up racing. Just as he knew it was his guilt that was causing the feelings rushing through him. For him to hang onto the only thing that kept him sane, he had to try to make amends.

No, racing wasn't the only thing that kept him sane. If he admitted nothing else, he would admit that.

Raven Blass kept him sane, made him laugh, made him feel things he hadn't felt in a long time. But for her sake he had to walk away. Keep walking away. He was toxic in this state.

He couldn't allow himself to be swayed into thinking he was anything else but what she'd first thought him to be.

As for what he planned to do… His father had summoned him.

Since he had nothing to lose, he saw no reason to refuse the summons. Just as he saw no reason to examine why his heart felt as if it would burst out of his chest with every step he took away from her.

Gritting his teeth, he walked out, threw a *'no comment'* to a stunned media before he stepped up in his helicopter and buckled himself in. He had no heart. So he had nothing to worry about.

Raven got the email an hour later. She'd been fired. Rafael de Cervantes no longer needed her services. She would be paid her full contract fee and an insanely hefty bonus for her inconvenience. Et cetera…et cetera…

Thing was, she wasn't surprised. Or even hurt. The man she'd fallen in love with was in full retreat mode because she'd got under his skin, had glimpsed the ravaged soul of the outwardly irreverent but desperately lonely playboy who had been grappling with monstrous demons.

She could've fought to stay, cited contract clauses and notice periods, but she knew first-hand how intransigent Rafael could be. And she knew offering her help when it was unwelcome would only set back the progress she'd made.

So she sent an email response. She would leave on one condition. That he let her recommend a physio who could help.

His curt text message agreeing to the condition made her heart contract painfully. Her next request was flatly refused.

No, Rafael stated, he had no wish to see her. But he wished her good luck with her future endeavours.

Raven watched the remaining All-Star events like most people did around the world—from the comfort of her couch. Except she had an extra reason to watch. She told herself she was making sure Rafael's new physio was doing a good enough job. It only took a glimpse of Rafael walking down the paddock en route to his car at the Montreal race to know that he hadn't suffered any setbacks.

At least not physically.

His haggard features told a different story. That and his studious avoidance of the media.

Her heart clenched as she devoured images of him; called herself ten kinds of fool when she froze his latest image and let her gaze settle on his hauntingly beautiful face.

The icy blue eyes staring into the camera still held the hint of devilish irreverence that was never far away but a raw desperation lurked there too, one that made tears prick her eyes. With a shaky hand, she pressed the release button and sat, numb, as the rest of the race unfolded.

Whatever Rafael had been running from still chased him with vicious relentlessness. The thought made her heart ache so painfully, she was halfway to picking up the phone when she stopped herself.

What would she say to him that she hadn't said before? He'd made it painfully clear he didn't want her interfering in his life. Like all his relationships, she'd been a means to an end, a sexual panacea to make him forget. She had no choice but to accept it was over.

She needed to put the past in the past and move on.

Which was why she nearly binned the invitation that arrived a week later.

The All-Star event's last race was taking place in Monaco. To be followed by an All-Star gala in honour of the drivers who'd given up their time to raise money for the road safety programme.

The only thing that stopped her from throwing the invitation away was the hand-written note from Sasha de Cervantes on behalf of her and her husband.

Sasha had been a good friend to her when she'd first joined the X1 Premier. Raven knew she'd put her friendship with Rafael on the line because of her and it had almost caused an irreparable rift between them. Certainly, she knew that not admitting Raven's role in Rafael's accident was what had caused the initial friction between Sasha and Marco.

So although attending the gala would mean she ran the risk of coming face to face with Rafael, Raven slid the invitation and the accompanying first class aeroplane ticket into her bag, then spent the next three days desperately trying to stop her heart from beating itself into exhaustion every time she thought of returning to Monaco.

Rafael stood before the door leading to the study at Casa León, where his father waited. Contrary to his intentions when he'd left Mexico two weeks ago, he hadn't made the trip to León. The indescribable need that had assailed him as he'd lifted off the racetrack in Mexico had led him down another path. A path which had brought him an infinitesimal amount of comfort. Comfort and the courage to grasp the door before him…and open it.

His father was seated behind his ancient desk in the room that seemed to have fallen into a time warp décor-wise.

'*Buenos tardes*, Papá.'

'*Mi hijo*,' his father replied. My son. 'It's good to see you.'

Guilt and sadness welled in Rafael's chest as he let his gaze rest properly on his father for the first time in eight years. His hair had turned almost completely grey and his limbs, paralysed thanks to Rafael, appeared shrunken. But his eyes, grey and sharp like Marco's, sparked with keen intellect and an expression Rafael thought he'd never see again. Or maybe it was just wishful thinking. 'Is it?' he asked, his throat tight with all the emotions he held within.

'It's always good to see you. I've missed you. I miss you every day.'

Rafael advanced into the room on shaky legs, inhaling an even shakier breath. 'How can you say that after all I've done?'

'What exactly do you think you've done, Rafa?'

He let out a harsh laugh and speared a hand through his hair. '*Por favor*, Papá. Condemn me to hell. It's where I belong, after all.'

'I think you've done a good job all by yourself. Now it's time to end this.'

'End this?'

His father nodded to a file on his desk. 'Sit down and read that.'

The hand he reached across the desk felt as feeble as a newborn's. The file contained a three-page report, one he read with growing disbelief.

'What is this?' he rasped through numb lips.

'It's the truth of what happened to your car that day, Rafael. You're not responsible for your mother's death.'

Shock hollowed his stomach. 'No…it can't be. Please tell me you're not making this up in some attempt to make me feel less guilty.'

'As your father, it's my duty to comfort you when you feel bad. It's also my duty to make you see the truth in front of your own eyes. You've been so bent on punishing yourself you've failed to listen to reason or contemplate the evidence. You told me when you first drove the car that you felt something wasn't right. That's what made your brother decide to investigate further. It turned out your hunch was right.'

'It says here all fifteen models of that car have been recalled for the same error. But it doesn't excuse the fact that I was running on fumes that day, high from partying even though my body was exhausted from being up almost twenty-four hours straight.'

'All things you'd been doing since you hit late puberty. All those things combined, while it gave me nightmares as a father, didn't make me think for a second that you would be dangerous behind a steering wheel or I wouldn't have bought you such a powerful machine, and I certainly wouldn't have allowed my beloved Ana in the car with you.'

The pure truth behind his father's words hit him square in the solar plexus. He stumbled backward and sagged onto the ancient leather armchair.

'I can't…I don't know what to say.' His head dropped into his hands and he felt tears prick his eyes.

'Let it go, Rafa. You've punished yourself enough over this. Your mamá wouldn't want this for you.'

The sob choked him, hot and tight and cathartic. Once it started, he couldn't seem to make it stop. He didn't even have the strength to lift his head when he heard the haunting whine of his father's wheelchair.

'Enough, son…enough.'

He looked up through a mist of tears. 'Forgive me, Papá.'

His father's smile touched him in a way that went beyond the physical. 'There's nothing to forgive. There never was.'

Footsteps sounded and Marco walked in, cradling his son, with Sasha right behind him.

She stopped dead when she saw him, her eyes widening in disbelief. 'Good grief, I never thought I'd live to see the day you'd be reduced to tears, Rafa. Quick, Marco, activate your phone's camera. We'll make a killing on YouTube.'

Marco laughed, their father snorted, even baby Jack chimed in with a hearty gurgle.

'So, we're all good here?' Marco asked several minutes later, his grey eyes probing as they darted between his father and his brother.

Rafael's gaze met his father's and the unconditional love he saw made the tightness in his chest give way just a tiny bit further. 'We're getting there.'

He had a feeling he'd never get there completely. Not while he felt a part of himself still missing.

'Pacing a crater through that carpet won't make the next few hours of your life any easier. You're screwed ten ways to Sunday. Accept that now and you'll be fine.'

Rafael glared at the amusement on his brother's face and clenched his fist. 'Don't you have an adoring wife somewhere who's waiting for you to swoon over her?' He walked over to the balcony overlooking the immense ballroom and scoured the crowd again, his stomach clenching when he didn't spot the figure he sought.

'Sí,' Marco replied smugly. 'But watching you twist yourself into knots is fun, too.'

'Keep it up and I'll be twisting my fist into your face.'

Marco grinned, an expression that had been rare in the years after his own personal tragedy of losing his unborn child. Sasha had brought the smile back to his brother's face. A smile that was now rubbing him a dozen different wrong ways.

As if he knew he was skating close to the edge, Marco sobered. 'If it helps, I messed up with Sasha, too.'

'It doesn't. Sasha is a soft touch. I'm not surprised she was fooled by those puppy-dog eyes of yours.'

Marco laughed. 'You're in more trouble than I thought if you're that deluded.' When his brother tapped him on the shoulder, Rafael was ready with a pithy response. Instead he saw Marco nod over his shoulder.

'Your Armageddon is here. I'd wish you luck but I've always thought you were dealt more than your fair share at birth. So I'll just suggest you don't balls it up...'

Rafael had stopped listening. His attention, his whole being was focused on the figure framed in the double doors of the ballroom.

Her black silky hair was caught up in a high, elaborate bun that made her sleek neck seem longer. And her dress, a simple but classy white gown threaded with gold sequined lines, followed her curves in a loving caress that made his mouth dry.

The vision of her, so stunning, so held together while he was falling apart inside, made his fingers tighten over the banister railing.

He watched Sasha approach and hug her. Her smile made his breath catch and, once again, Rafael felt a bolt of dismay at the thought of what he'd thrown away.

A waiter offered her a glass of champagne. She was about to take a sip when her gaze rose and collided with his.

The force of emotion that shot through him galvanised his frozen feet. He was moving along the balcony and the stairs before he'd taken a full breath.

Sasha saw him approach, gave him a stern *don't-mess-this-up-or-I'll-castrate-you* look and melted away into the crowd. Raven made no move to walk away, and he wasn't sure whether he was relieved or disturbed because her face gave nothing away.

No pleasure. No censure. Just a careful social mask that made his heart twist.

'You're late.' Ah, *brava*, Rafa. *Brava*.

'My flight out of London was delayed due to fog. I explained to Sasha. She's forgiven me.'

The not-so-subtle barb found its mark. *I'm not here for you.*

He wanted to touch, wanted to feel the warmth of her skin so badly, he had to swallow several times before he could speak.

'I need to talk to you.'

Her eyes widened. 'Why? I thought you said all you had to say in Mexico.'

He tried for a careless shrug. 'Perhaps I have a few more things to say.'

She glanced away and gave her still-full glass to a passing waiter. 'I don't want to hear it. We were never friends, not really. And you fired me from being your physio. That leaves us nothing in common.'

'I'm seeing a therapist,' he blurted out.

Shocked eyes returned to his. 'You are?'

His smile felt false and painful. 'Yes, I figured I must be the only high-profile figure without the requisite head-shrinker as an accessory. Now I'm a fully fledged, card-carrying whack-job. But I still want to talk to you.'

She pressed lightly glossed lips together and shook her head. 'I don't think it's a good idea.'

Feeling the ground rock under him, he reached out and captured her wrist. 'You were right.'

Her breath caught. 'About what?' she whispered.

He started to answer but a burst of laughter from nearby guests stopped him. 'Not here.' He pulled her towards the doors and breathed in relief when she didn't resist. The lift ride up to his VIP suite was made in silence. After shutting the door, he threw his key card on a nearby table and shrugged off his tuxedo jacket.

'You were right about everything.'

She turned from the window overlooking the stunning marina. Her gaze slid over him, a hasty assessment which nevertheless made the blood thrum in his veins.

'Even I can't take responsibility for *everything.*'

'According to my shrink, I'm suffering from a combination of survivor's guilt and PTSD. Together, they make for one sexy but volatile cocktail of emotions.'

She licked her lips then curved them into a quick smile. An impersonal smile. She started to move towards the door. 'Well, I'm happy that you're getting some help. If that's all, I'll return downstairs. I don't wish to be rude to Sasha—'

'I also spoke to my father.'

She froze. He took advantage of her hesitation and stalked after her. Catching her around the waist, he pulled her body into his. She gave the tiniest gasp but didn't fight to get away.

Rafael took that as a good sign. 'I finally flew to León and spoke to my father.' He gave her the gist of their family meeting.

'Why are you telling me all this, Rafael?' she whispered.

He pulled her closer until he felt the sweet curve of her bottom against his groin. For a quick second, he lost himself in her scent, breathed her in and let her warm his frozen soul. The past three weeks had shown him there was an even worse hell than the one he'd previously inhabited. Because in that one he'd lost Raven.

Hell without Raven was a whole new reality. One he was desperate to escape.

'You made me face up to my flaws, to seek help before I hurt anyone else.' He couldn't stop himself from brushing his lips against her nape.

Her delicate shudder gave him hope but her next words dashed them completely. 'So you wanted to thank me? I accept your gratitude. Let me go, please.'

He held on tight. 'I'm seeking help, Raven, learning to change. But I need you. Without you, all this will be for nothing.'

She finally turned in his arms. The look on her face threatened to stop his breath. 'You can't do this because of me. You should want to seek help for yourself.'

'*Sí*, even I get that. But nothing I do will have any meaning unless you're part of that change.'

'What exactly are you saying?' she whispered.

Go for broke, Rafa. Hell, there was nothing left to lose. No, scratch that. There was everything to lose. Without her, his life had no meaning. So he took the biggest gamble he'd ever taken.

'*Lo siento*. I got it horribly wrong. I'm sorry.'

'What did you get wrong?'

'Not seeing the treasure I had in you until it was too late.'

She shook her head and grimaced. 'I'm no treasure, Rafael. I am just as damaged as you. I fooled myself into thinking a half-life was better than letting myself feel. You made me see that I'd let my father's treatment of me cloud my judgement so I pushed everyone away.'

His hand tightened on her waist. 'You know what I want to do?'

She shook her head.

'I want to track him down and ram my fist so far down his throat, he'll never speak again.'

'Don't let your shrink hear you say that.'

His smile felt grim and tight. 'I said I was trying to change. I never said I was aiming for saint of the year.' He sobered. 'I'm disgusted that my behaviour brought up what happened to you when you lived with him.'

'That's just it. Deep down I knew you were nothing like him but I'd programmed myself so thoroughly I let myself grasp the excuse when everyone told me you were nothing but a ruthless playboy.'

'And of course I went out of my way to prove them right.'

'If you were, you'd never have agreed to stop flirting with other women. Never have refused Chantilly's blatant invitation.'

Raven saw the flash of self-disgust and pain in his eyes.

'There was a time when I wouldn't have.'

'Past tense. You're a better man now. A better person.'

'Because of you.' His knuckle brushed down her cheek in a gesture so soft and gentle, tears threatened.

Despite the foolish hope that threatened, Raven's heart remained frozen. She couldn't remain here. If she did, she'd end up making a total fool of herself.

'I have to go—'

'I love you,' he rasped in a whisper so fierce it sizzled around the room.

'I…*what?*'

His heartbreakingly beautiful face contorted in a grimace. 'I'm still broken, *querida*, not so much on the outside any more, but I'm a long way from being perfect. And I know it's selfish of me but I want you so very desperately that I have to ask you to consider taking a chance on me, flawed and hideous as I am.' Acute vulnerability shone from his eyes and, when he grasped her arms, Raven felt the tremor in his fingers.

'You love me?'

'I have no right to, and I can't promise that I won't be a complete bastard on occasion, but *sí*, I love you. And I'll do anything to make you agree to hitch a ride with this broken wagon.'

'Rafael…'

He kissed her silent, as if he was afraid of what she'd say. She kissed him back, infusing every single drop of what she felt into the act. Somehow, he got the message.

He pulled back sharply, the question blazing its intensity in his eyes.

'Yes, my gorgeous man. I love you too.'

A frenzied tearing of clothes followed that sweet, soul-shaking confession. They made love right there in the living room, on the plush, expensive rug helpfully supplied by the five-star hotel.

She held her breath as Rafael slid on the sheath and prowled his naked body over hers. Hardly believing that this beautiful man was hers, she caressed her fingers down his firm cheek. He turned his head and kissed her palm, then, being the shameless opportunist he was, he kissed his way down her arm to her shoulder, then over her chest to capture one rigid nipple in his mouth.

At the same time, he parted her thighs with his and entered her in one bold thrust. Their coupling was fast, furious, their need for each other a raging fire that swiftly burned out of control.

When they'd caught their breaths, Rafael moved, picked her up and walked her into the bedroom.

'Should you be doing that?' she asked.

'I'm a renewed man. I can move mountains.' He let go of her and she tumbled onto the bed. Before she got totally lost in the effortlessly skilled seduction she knew he was aiming her way, she placed a hand on his lips.

'We haven't talked about your racing.'

His settled his long frame next to hers, his eyes serious. 'I think I need to concentrate on getting myself mentally in shape before I get behind the wheel. I've turned down a seat for this season.'

Knowing what it must have taken for him to turn down what he loved doing, her heart swelled. 'You take care of the mental aspect. I'll make sure your body is whipped into shape in time for next year's season.'

He grinned and tugged her close. 'I'd expect no less from my take-no-prisoners future wife.'

Her breath stalled. 'Is that a proposal, Rafael?'

'It's whatever you want it to be. If you don't think I'll make a good enough husband, you can take me as your sex slave. Or your boy toy. Or your f—'

She stopped him with a kiss before he finished. His incorrigible laugh promised retribution. And, for the life of her, Raven couldn't think of a better way to be punished.

'Sasha is going to hate me for disappearing from her gala,' she said an hour later.

'No, she's not. I begged her to send you the invitation. We both agreed I owe her big.'

She mock glared at him. 'You're right, you haven't changed one little bit.'

He laughed, a rich sound that made her soul sing. When he stared deep into her eyes her heart turned over. 'I have something to show you.'

Curious, she watched him reach into his drawer and pull out a sheaf of papers.

'You finished it?'

'Yes,' he answered. There was no laughter in his voice, no shameless lust monster lurking behind the stunning blue eyes.

There was only a careful, almost painfully hopeful expectancy.

She took the papers from him. Seeing the one word title, her heart caught—*Mamá*.

'I knew it. I knew Ana and Carlos were your parents.'

Two hours later, she looked up, tears streaming down her face. He'd sat with her back tucked against his front, in watchful silence while she read, all the while knowing he'd been reading his words alongside her.

The sheen of tears in his eyes rocked her soul.

'It's beautiful, Rafael.'

'*Gracias.* I hope, wherever she is, she forgives me for what I did.'

'She's your mother. That's what mothers do. And I promise to remind you of that whenever the nightmares threaten.'

The look in his eyes made hers fill all over again. '*Mi corazon.* I don't deserve you.'

Her smile was watery. 'No, you don't. But I'll let you have me anyway.'

EPILOGUE

'SO WHAT DO I get for winning the bet?' Raven asked as they stood in another luxurious room, surrounded by well-heeled guests, the very best vintage champagne and excellent food.

'What more could you possibly want, *mi amor*? You have my slavish adoration by day and my hot body by night.'

'Yes, but do you know how draining it's been to reassure you every day for the last three months that your book will be a smashing success? That more than one person will turn up at this launch?'

Rafael mock frowned. 'Have I been that needy?'

'Yes, you have, but don't think I wasn't fooled by what that neediness got you. You owe me big.'

'I seem to owe everyone big. Okay, how about…' He whispered a very hot, very dirty suggestion of payment. She was still blushing several minutes later when they both heard the whine of an electric wheelchair.

Rafael's father stopped beside them. An electronic copy of Rafael's book had been programmed into a tablet on his wheelchair, and the front page showed a picture of Rafael's mother, her face creased in a stunning smile as she laughed into the camera.

Rafael told her he'd taken that picture the year before she died.

'Carlos, please tell your son to stop worrying about his book. He thinks one of us has been bribing the critics to give it rave reviews.'

Carlos smiled and glanced at his son. Then he started to speak to him in Spanish. Slowly, Rafael's smile disappeared until his face was transformed into a look of intense love and gratitude. With a shaky hand, he touched his father's shoulder, then bent forward and kissed both his cheeks.

'*Gracias,* Papá.' His voice was rough as he straightened.

Carlos nodded, his own eyes holding a sheen of tears as he rolled his chair away.

'What did he say?'

'He's proud of me. And my mother would be too if she were here.'

As hard as she blinked, the tears welled. 'Damn it, you de Cervantes men sure know how to ruin a girl's make up.'

He caught her around the waist and pulled her close into his hard body.

'You're now a de Cervantes too. You can't take back your vows.'

She gave a mock grimace. She was still getting used to her new name, just as she was getting used to wearing the exquisite engagement and wedding ring set that had belonged to Rafael's mother. 'Raven de Cervantes is such a mouthful.'

'Hmm…' He nuzzled her neck, instantly melting her insides. 'We could shorten it.'

'You mean like just initials or a symbol like that rock star?'

'Not quite.'

'What have you in mind?' she asked, her fingers toying with buttons she couldn't wait to undo later. The promise of exploring the flesh underneath made her hot.

He worked along her jaw until he reached the side of her mouth. With a whisper-soft kiss, he raised his head and looked directly into her eyes. 'How about just…*amor querida*?'

Her heart, her soul and the rest of her body melted into him.

When his thumb brushed her cheek, she blinked back tears.

'That works. That works very well for me.'

* * * * *

Merry Christmas
& A Happy New Year!

Thank you for a wonderful
2013...

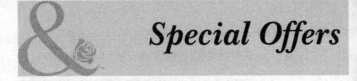

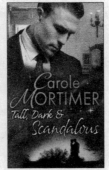
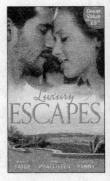

Come in from the cold this Christmas with two of
our favourite authors. Whether you're jetting off to
Vermont with Sarah Morgan or settling down for
Christmas dinner with Fiona Harper, the smiles
won't stop this festive season.

Visit:
www.millsandboon.co.uk

Join the Mills & Boon Book Club

**Want to read more Modern™ books?
We're offering you 2 more absolutely FREE!**

We'll also treat you to these fabulous extras:

- 🌹 **Exclusive offers and much more!**

- 🌹 **FREE home delivery**

- 🌹 **FREE books and gifts with our special rewards scheme**

Get your free books now!

**visit www.millsandboon.co.uk/bookclub
or call Customer Relations on 020 8288 2888**